Half a Day
AND OTHER STORIES

An ANTHOLOGY of SHORT STORIES from NORTH EASTERN and EASTERN AFRICA

Selection and introduction
Ayebia Clarke

MACMILLAN
KENYA

© Copyright text Macmillan Kenya Publishers Ltd, 2004

© Copyright illustrations Macmillan Kenya Publishers Ltd, 2004

Selection and introduction by Ayebia Clarke

All rights reserved. No reproduction, copy or transmission of this publication may be made without written permission.

No paragraph of this publication may be reproduced, copied or transmitted save with written permission or in accordance with the provisions of the Copyright, Designs and Patents Act 1988, or under the terms of any licence permitting limited copying issued by the Copyright Licensing Agency, 90 Tottenham Court Road, London W1P 9HE.

Any person who does any unauthorised act in relation to this publication may be liable to criminal prosecution and civil claims for damages.

First published 2004 by
MACMILLAN KENYA PUBLISHERS LTD
Kijabe Street
PO Box 30797
Nairobi

ISBN 9966-34-085-8

10 9 8 7 6 5 4 3 2 1
13 12 11 10 09 08 07 06 05 04

This book is printed on paper suitable for recycling and made from fully managed and sustainable forest sources.

Printed and bound in Nairobi by English Press Ltd.

Illustrations by Kennedy Kimeu

Cover illustration by David Axtell
Cover design by Charles Design Associates

All rights reserved by Macmillan Publishers Ltd.

Contents

INTRODUCTION	1
HALF A DAY *Naguib Mahfouz – Egypt*	7
THE TOWN *Eneriko Seruma – Uganda*	13
MONEYMAN *Peter Nazareth – Uganda*	20
THE MARTYR *Ngugi wa Thiong'o – Kenya*	27
A MEETING IN THE DARK *Ngugi wa Thiong'o – Kenya*	37
LETTER TO MY SISTERS *Fatmata Conteh – Ethiopia*	51
SOLITUDE *Nawal El Saadawi – Egypt*	63
AGAINST THE PLEASURE PRINCIPLE *Saida Hagi-Dirie Herzi – Somalia*	70
GOVERNMENT BY MAGIC SPELL *Saida Hagi-Dirie Herzi – Somalia*	78
WHO CARES FOR THE NEW MILLENNIUM? *Hama Tuma – Ethiopia*	85
HEAVEN AND EARTH *Wangui wa Goro – Kenya*	91
ON THE MARKET DAY *Kyalo Mativo – Kenya*	104
THE HANDS OF THE BLACKS *Luis Bernado Honwana – Mozambique*	115
BREAKING LOOSE *Moyez G. Vassanji – Kenya*	120

Acknowledgements

The publisher and editor wish to thank the following rights holders for the use of copyright material:

Hama Tuma for 'Who cares for New Millennium?' by Hama Tuma; Doubleday Broadway Publishing Group for 'Half a day' from *The time and the place and other stories* by Naguib Mahfouz, copyright 1991 by the American University in Cairo Press, used by permission of Doubleday, a division of Random House, Inc; Peter Nazareth for "Moneyman" by Peter Nazareth; Watkins/Loomis Agency for permission to reprint 'A Meeting in the Dark' and 'The Martyr' from *Secret Lives* by Ngugi Wa Thiong'o; Swedish International Development Cooperation Agency (SIDA) for 'Letter to my sisters' by Fatmata Conteth from *Whispering Land*, an anthology of stories by African women, SIDA, 1985; Wangui wa Goro for 'Heaven and Earth' by Wangui wa Goro; A P Watt on behalf of Luis Bernado Honwana for 'The Hands of the Blacks' by Luis Bernado Honwana; Heinemann Education for 'Breaking loose' from *Uhuru Street* by M G Vassanji

If any copyright holders have been omitted, please contact the publishers who will make the necessary arrangements at the first opportunity.

Introduction

Oral and written traditions

Since the beginning of time, people have made sense of the world by telling stories. Storytelling has been the way to shape experience, give it a meaning, explain and record events. Around fires, cooking pots and tables, communities have gathered for centuries to keep alive the collective memories, legends, myths and heroic adventures of their people.

The storyteller's calling was a sacred art – the power of narrating was closely linked to magic. Stories were sung or acted out, or recited to the accompaniment of music or drumming. The storyteller was a highly skilled person – he had to entertain his audience, keep their attention, create suspense, as well as preserve tradition and weave a magic spell. The relation of narrator to his audience was of prime importance.

When stories were written down for the first time they became hardened into a set form. The speaker (narrator) and audience disappeared, becoming author and reader, and the written text became the focus. The whole drama of storytelling became the solitary, (often) silent act of one individual. The epic – the long poetic form about the adventures of a hero – stiffened into prose, later the novel, while songs, ballads and rhymes accompanied by music and drums, became what we now call poetry. In cultures where writing appeared later, the oral tradition still flavours the written word: the storyteller is still alive and the audience still a communal ear. In Africa particularly, literature is an exciting and ever-changing discipline. Many writers try to keep an oral flavour in their writing. Instead of imitating a 'Western' style, they retain some elements of African traditions of narrations. As readers, then, we are asked not simply to read, analyse and critique the stories but to respect the calling of the ancient storyteller, to listen and participate in the act of storytelling.

The short story

The short story was a late developer in literature. By the thirteenth century, drama and poetry had established themselves as recognisable forms. The novel became possible with the development of the printing press, and became a popular form in the eighteenth century. But the short story only began to appear in the early nineteenth century. In Europe, the Russian writers Chekhov and Tolstoy began writing and publishing well-structured short tales. In North America, Edgar Allan Poe published his *Tales of Mystery and Imagination*, calling them a new 'form' of literature. Poe claimed that, unlike a novel, the short story was a narrative that could be read 'at one sitting'. He also argued that the short story had a 'unit of purpose' the novel didn't have – it had to create a 'single effect'. It had to be efficient and economic in words and plot, using few characters and focusing on one single event to make its point.

Introduction

Contrary to what we might expect, the short story is considered to be the most difficult genre to write, because of the concentration and condensation needed. Everything – every word, detail, character – must have purpose and work to a final end. Whereas a novel can wander through many scenes, characters, sub-plots, resolutions and conflicts, the short story must be to the point: one conflict, one climax, one resolution.

The short story in Africa

In spite of the difficulty in writing the short story, it has become the most popular form of literature in Africa today. There are many reasons for this:

● *Brevity*

The idea of reading a story 'at one sitting' makes the short story most suited to the readers whose leisure time is limited. Some readers who only have short snatches of time to read, on the way to and from work, prefer poetry and short stories that are to the point, immediately accessible, and concentrated. Many African writers are journalists, trained to make their point effective and quickly, so the short story genre appeals to them, too. Practically speaking, the short story can also find a publisher more easily than a novel because of its brevity. There are many places a short story can be published – a newspaper, magazine, journal – without a great deal of expense.

● *Subject matter*

It has been argued that the short story is the best way to present short 'snapshots' of real life. Writers often talk of writing short stories that portray 'life as it is'. Often too, there is a political point to be made. Politics move quickly, and a novel written to protest about some contemporary issue quickly becomes outdated, sometimes before it is even published. In apartheid South Africa in the 1950s, authors writing for the *Drum*[1] realised this, and developed the short story genre into a fast, accessible form of protest.

● *Oral tradition*

Many people think that the short story is the ideal medium for the oral tradition. The short story resembles an oral tale in that it has to be read (heard) in one sitting, and the storyteller must hold the attention of the audience for the duration of the entire story. African writers have often chosen the short story to communicate and express an oral style. Even writers who are primarily novelists use the short story as their apprenticeship into the craft of writing. The short story, even if not easier to write, has been easier to publish and easier to read than a novel, and has grown into an exciting art form.

Characterisation

Character in literature is the always shifting and changing element that makes each story different no matter how similar the plot. Character pumps the heart of fiction. It is character, and the 'love and honour and pity and pride and compassion and sacrifice' characters experience, that carries news from their world to ours. Characterisation is the central thread that knits the story together and stops it from falling apart. In Saida Hagi-Dirie Herzi's *Against the Pleasure Principle*, Rahma's character is very strong in putting her case, in opposition to the pressure from her mother and the extended family, against female circumcision. Similarly, in Ngugi's *A Meeting in the Dark*, John, the central character, is the sustaining factor of the storyline; but even towards the end of the story when his character begins to falter – his strength and endurance has already been established and the reader is drawn to him in sympathy.

Narrative techniques

African short stories are written as if they are meant for performance, for group interaction or for communal engagement and enjoyment. Often the writer uses the oral narrative style to fit the written form, mimicking the storyteller's craft in speaking to an imaginary audience. To make it more accessible, the writer's use of language is closely aligned to the spoken word, that is to say he or she uses English language with an African expression or what is known as an African idiom. In other instances, to authenticate the text, the writer may use the narrative voice to substitute words that are not transferable into English with African language expressions as a way of finding a point of connection with the audience. For example in Ngugi's *A Meeting in the Dark*, he describes a scene about a woman carrying a load: 'she was carrying a big load of *Kuni* which bent her into an *Akamba*-bow shape.' The words *Kuni* and *Akamba* are clearly Kenyan language expressions used to authenticate the story and set it firmly in an African mode. Similarly the use of the word, *hei!* carries connotations of surprise and common currency in many African languages.

Point of view

In any discussion of how writers create characters, their point of view is an important concern. At its most basic level, point of view can simply be thought of as the perception of the character that is held in the eye of the camera. Through the eyes or direction of the narrator we view or experience the story.

Third person – the omniscient narrator

This narrative style puts a distance between the writer and his or her subject. It can offer the writer a way to see beyond what the character can see. Third person also allows the writer more freedom in the use of language. The omniscient narrator is the all-seeing and all-knowing narrative voice who is able to describe the emotions, behaviour and motivations of every character and can foretell their thoughts and actions from beginning to end.

The first person – the 'I' voice

The first person narrative technique is by its nature subjective, the speaker is the subject – even if the story seems to be about someone or something else. An observer who is also a participant in the unfolding action, and will be involved with events of the story in such a way that the outcome will affect his or her life directly, is the central character: as, for example, in El Saadawi's *Solitude*.

Themes

A cursory examination of African writing reveals that writers have tended to engage with the social, political and moral issues of the day. In the beginning, writers confronted the realities of the clash of cultures but recent literature has shifted the focus to cultures at crossroads and the struggle between European and African traditions for authority and for the power to define what is central, and the marginalised. Modern African writing is currently engaged with questions of tradition versus modernity, crumbling and corruptive social structures and urban and rural imperatives vying for position and resources, and the position of women and children in society. The phrase that captures the collective concerns of the ordinary person which runs through the collection is 'struggle for emancipation in modern Africa'.

The themes in this collection are as wide ranging as the authors' backgrounds, countries of origin, religious beliefs and gender but share a common belief – a concern for justice and a more democratically structured society that disapproves of any form of discrimination. *The Martyr* and *The Hands of the Blacks* represent stories focusing on racial discrimination in the colonial era in African society. The stories also reveal the communal nature of the communities where family, clan and neighbourhood ties are important, central and valued above personal or individual relationships. In *The Martyr*, the central protagonist's disloyalty to his kinsmen eventually results in his downfall, as the outsider he is secretly protecting is the very person who unknowingly kills him.

Corruption and dictatorships

Three stories examine the era of corrupt regimes and recurring dictatorships and the impact of this on the people. In *Government by Magic Spell*, the narrator invites us to a form of gathering and tells an imaginary audience about the gradual and unhurried disintegration of society with a detached air of authority and ends the story on a note of caution. The story hinges on the main protagonist and the details of the unfolding disaster are narrated with a knowing air and self assurance in a way that resembles a village elder addressing a kinship gathering. At the basic level, *On the Market Day* is a story about extreme poverty, misfortune and hopelessness. The narrator provides us with a living history written in straightforward, simple and direct language explaining what is happening but does not tell the reader what to think, or claim any credit. Instead, he presents the facts and leaves the reader to make up his or her own mind. *Who Cares for the New Millennium*, on the other hand, is a satirical take on African dictatorships – it is a more direct social commentary that reminds the reader of the forces levelled against Africa which have resulted in its lowly position in the new world order. It mocks an imaginary audience about their complicity by inaction as a device to shock them into action.

Feminist narratives

Four stories stand out in this collection as a tribute to women's writing, courage and their enduring strength in the face of entrenched patriarchal power and authority in African societies. *Heaven and Earth* exposes the taboo subject of domestic violence (especially against women), often under reported; the story underplays the importance of the main character and situates the narrative in a religious setting to give it more power, and an air of collusion in the collective silence the community is engaged in. *Letter to my Sisters* and *Solitude* are strongly feminist in their condemnation and questioning of the subjugation of women in Islamic societies in Africa. Nawal El Saadawi's writing is deeply rooted in Islamic culture from her Egyptian background and yet it is the questioning of this very background and society's unequal treatment of women that has earned her notoriety in her country and in many court battles against hard-line Islamic believers. In *Against the Pleasure Principle*, traditional beliefs and modern practices clash in the hotly debated topic of female circumcision. This story reveals the deep and often damaging divisions between the older and younger members of society – about tradition versus modern scientific discoveries that reject traditional practices – which now threaten to divide the community.

Family relationships

The theme of family relationships runs though almost every story in this collection. The stories paint pictures of traditional family settings in diverse situations, often challenged and interwoven with community spirit and support which has been passed down from generation to generation. In Naguib Mahfouz's story, *Half a Day*, a child's awakening and the innocence of the child narrator's voice and point of view predominate. Because we trust a child's perspective, the reader journeys with the character to its natural conclusion – the realisation of new knowledge. In Peter Nazareth's story, *Moneyman*, we are shown the opposite side of the story where there appears to be the beginnings of a breakdown in family ties and relationships as a precursor to the breakdown of society. Leitao, the main protagonist, exploits poor and lowly paid African civil servants by lending them money at exorbitant rates of interest and gets away with it. He decides to extend his usury to the larger community with disastrous consequences. *Moneyman* is a classic case in point where greed and selfishness, the story warns, are rewarded with loneliness and isolation.

This anthology brings together writers from varied backgrounds representing the true and changing phase of African writing. It spans the length and breadth of the continent in its diversity of styles, themes, interests, points of view and locations. There is a variety of topics – personal, communal, political and social aspects of daily life experience. The range of stories spans the historical, as well as contemporary issues. It includes stories written in the early 1960s with the start of the African Writers Series and translations from the former French and Portuguese colonies as well as a range of styles in English that deal with the complexities of African society. Between the covers you will visit some interesting worlds: the world of political intrigue and snobbery, the world of poverty and deprivation, and the uncompromising voice(s) of women in communities struggling to break free from this poverty and deprivation, patriarchal oppression and violence against women.

Some of the contributors to this anthology were arrested and imprisoned for long or short periods for their views and beliefs which were at variance with those in power at the time: both European colonialists and ruthless despots from independent Africa, who wanted to silence them. Some of the fragments of prison experiences gathered here have historical relevance as they constitute a defiant recasting of Africa's history through the eyes of some of its finest writers.

Breaking new ground always provokes ridicule. Recently, mostly young, self-motivated people have created a space for themselves in adverse economies by being innovative all over Africa. They seek to entertain, provoke and create. This anthology is a tribute to the courage and perseverance of African writers who continue to risk their lives and write about new worlds as a way of offering people the opportunity of opening up a dialogue for possible change.

Ayebia Clarke, December 2003.

Notes

1. *Drum* is a popular weekly black magazine in South Africa which publishes short fiction and poetry along with other features.

Naguib Mahfouz
Egypt

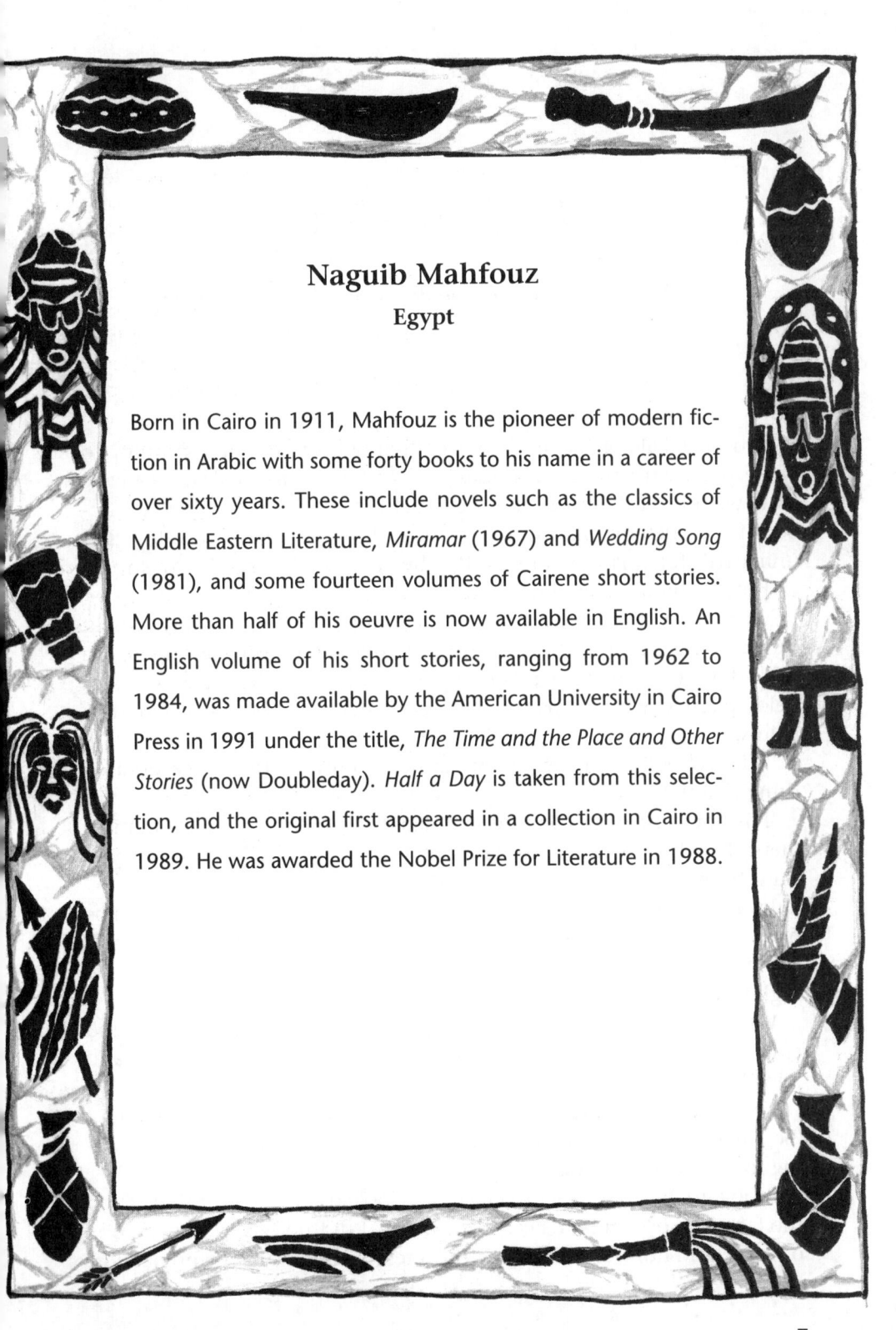

Born in Cairo in 1911, Mahfouz is the pioneer of modern fiction in Arabic with some forty books to his name in a career of over sixty years. These include novels such as the classics of Middle Eastern Literature, *Miramar* (1967) and *Wedding Song* (1981), and some fourteen volumes of Cairene short stories. More than half of his oeuvre is now available in English. An English volume of his short stories, ranging from 1962 to 1984, was made available by the American University in Cairo Press in 1991 under the title, *The Time and the Place and Other Stories* (now Doubleday). *Half a Day* is taken from this selection, and the original first appeared in a collection in Cairo in 1989. He was awarded the Nobel Prize for Literature in 1988.

Half a Day

(Translated from the Arabic by Denys Tohnson-Davies)

I proceeded alongside my father, clutching his right hand, running to keep up with the long strides he was taking. All my clothes were new: the black shoes, the green school uniform and the red tarboosh. My delight in my new clothes, however, was not altogether unmarred, for this was no feast day but the day on which I was to be cast into school for the first time.

My mother stood at the window watching our progress, and I would turn towards her from time to time, as though appealing for help. We walked along a street lined with gardens; on both sides were extensive fields planted with crops, prickly pears, henna trees and a few date palms.

'Why school?' I challenged my father openly. 'I shall never do anything to annoy you.'

'I'm not punishing you,' he said, laughing. 'School is not a punishment. It is the factory that makes useful men out of boys. Don't you want to be like your father and brothers?'

I was not convinced. I did not believe there was really any good to be had in tearing me away from the intimacy of my home and throwing me into this building that stood at the end of the road like some huge, high-walled fortress, exceedingly stern and grim.

When we arrived at the gate we could see the courtyard, vast and crammed full of boys and girls. 'Go in by yourself,' said my father, 'and join them. Put a smile on your face and be a good example to others.'

I hesitated and clung to his hand, but he gently pushed me from him. 'Be a man,' he said. 'Today you truly begin life. You will find me waiting for you when it's time to leave.'

I took a few steps, then stopped and looked but saw nothing. Then the faces of boys and girls came into view. I did not know a single one of them, and none of them knew me. I felt I was a stranger who had lost

Naguib Mahfouz

his way. But glances of curiosity were directed towards me, and one boy approached and asked, 'Who brought you?'

'My father,' I whispered.

'My father's dead,' he said quite simply.

I did not know what to say. The gate was closed, letting out a pitiable screech. Some of the children burst into tears. The bell rang. A lady came along, followed by a group of men. The men began sorting us into ranks. We were formed into an intricate pattern in the great courtyard surrounded on three sides by high buildings of several floors; from each floor we were overlooked by a long balcony roofed in wood.

'This is your new home,' said the woman. 'Here too there are mothers and fathers. Here there is everything that is enjoyable and beneficial to knowledge and religion. Dry your tears and face life joyfully.'

We submitted to the facts, and this submission brought a sort of contentment. Living beings were drawn to other living beings, and from the first moments my heart made friends with such boys as were to be my friends and fell in love with such girls as I was to be in love with, so that it seemed my misgivings had had no basis. I had never imagined school would have this rich variety. We played all sorts of different games: swings, the vaulting horse, ball games. In the music room we chanted our first songs. We also had our first introduction to language. We saw a globe of the Earth, which revolved and showed the various continents and countries. We started learning the numbers. The story of the Creator of the universe was read to us, we were told of His present world and of His Hereafter, and we heard examples of what He said. We ate delicious food, took a little nap and woke up to go on with friendship and love, play and learning.

As our path revealed itself to us, however, we did not find it as totally sweet and unclouded as we had presumed. Dust-laden winds and unexpected accidents came about suddenly, so we had to be watchful, at the ready and very patient. It was not all a matter of playing and fooling around. Rivalries could bring about pain and hatred or give rise to fighting. And while the lady would sometimes smile, she would often scowl and scold. Even more frequently she would resort to physical punishment.

In addition, the time for changing one's mind was over and gone and there was no question of ever returning to the paradise of home. Nothing lay ahead of us but exertion, struggle and perseverance. Those who were able took advantage of the opportunities for success and happiness that presented themselves amid the worries.

The bell rang announcing the passing of the day and the end of work. The throngs of children rushed towards the gate, which was opened again. I bade farewell to friends and sweethearts and passed through the gate. I peered around but found no trace of my father, who had promised to be there. I stepped aside to wait. When I had waited for a long time without avail, I decided to return home on my own. After I had taken a few steps, a middle-aged man passed by and I realised at once that I knew him. He came towards me, smiling, and shook me by the hand, saying, 'It's a long time since we last met – how are you?'

With a nod of my head, I agreed with him and in turn asked, 'And you, how are you?'

'As you can see, not all that good, the Almighty be praised!'

Again he shook me by the hand and went off. I proceeded a few steps, then came to a startled halt. Good Lord! Where was the street lined with gardens? Where had it disappeared to? When did all these vehicles invade it? And when did all these hordes of humanity come to rest upon its surface? How did these hills of refuse come to cover its sides? And where were the fields that bordered it? High buildings had taken over, the street surged with children and disturbing noises shook the air. At various points stood conjurors showing off their tricks and making snakes appear from baskets. Then there was a band announcing the opening of a circus, with clowns and weight lifters walking in front. A line of trucks carrying central security troops crawled majestically by. The siren of a fire engine shrieked, and it was not clear how the vehicle would cleave its way to reach the blazing fire. A battle raged between a taxi driver and his passenger, while the passenger's wife called out for help and no one answered. Good God! I was in a daze. My head spun. I almost went crazy. How could all this have happened in half a day, between early morning and sunset? I would find the answer at home with my father. But where was my home? I could see only tall buildings and hordes of people. I hastened on to the crossroads between the gardens and Abu Khoda. I had to cross Abu Khoda to reach my house, but the stream of cars would not let up. The fire engine's siren was shrieking at full pitch as it moved at a snail's pace, and I said to myself, 'Let the fire take its pleasure in what it consumes.' Extremely irritated, I wondered when I would be able to cross. I stood there a long time, until the young lad employed at the ironing shop on the corner came up to me. He stretched out his arm and said gallantly, 'Grandpa, let me take you across.'

Revision questions
1 a) Pick as many words and phrases as possible from the first eight paragraphs that show that the narrator did not at first like school.
   b) Explain how any four of them describe his feelings.
2 a) Describe the differences the narrator notes in the street on the way to school and on the way back home.

b) How do the differences reflect the change in the narrator's experiences?
3 What changed the narrator's attitude towards school?
4 'Nothing lay ahead of us but *exertion, struggle* and *perseverance*.'
   Explain the meanings of each of these words in the context of:
   a) one's school experiences
   b) growing up.
5 a) The characters who develop in this story are the *narrator* and the *lady* or *woman* who receives him in school. Describe each of them.
   b) Other characters like the narrator's father and the boy who helps the narrator cross the road do not develop fully but they play important roles in the narrator's life. Explain:
      (i) their literal role
      (ii) their symbolic role.

Topics for discussion
1 This story is told in the child narrator's voice, bringing out facts candidly, calmly and simply. Would it have been different if it had been a description?
2 Would you agree that 'school is the factory that makes useful men out of boys'? Explain.
3 a) How do the narrator's experiences of the first day in school symbolise an entire lifetime?
   b) Your answer in (a) should bring out the theme of the story. What is the theme?

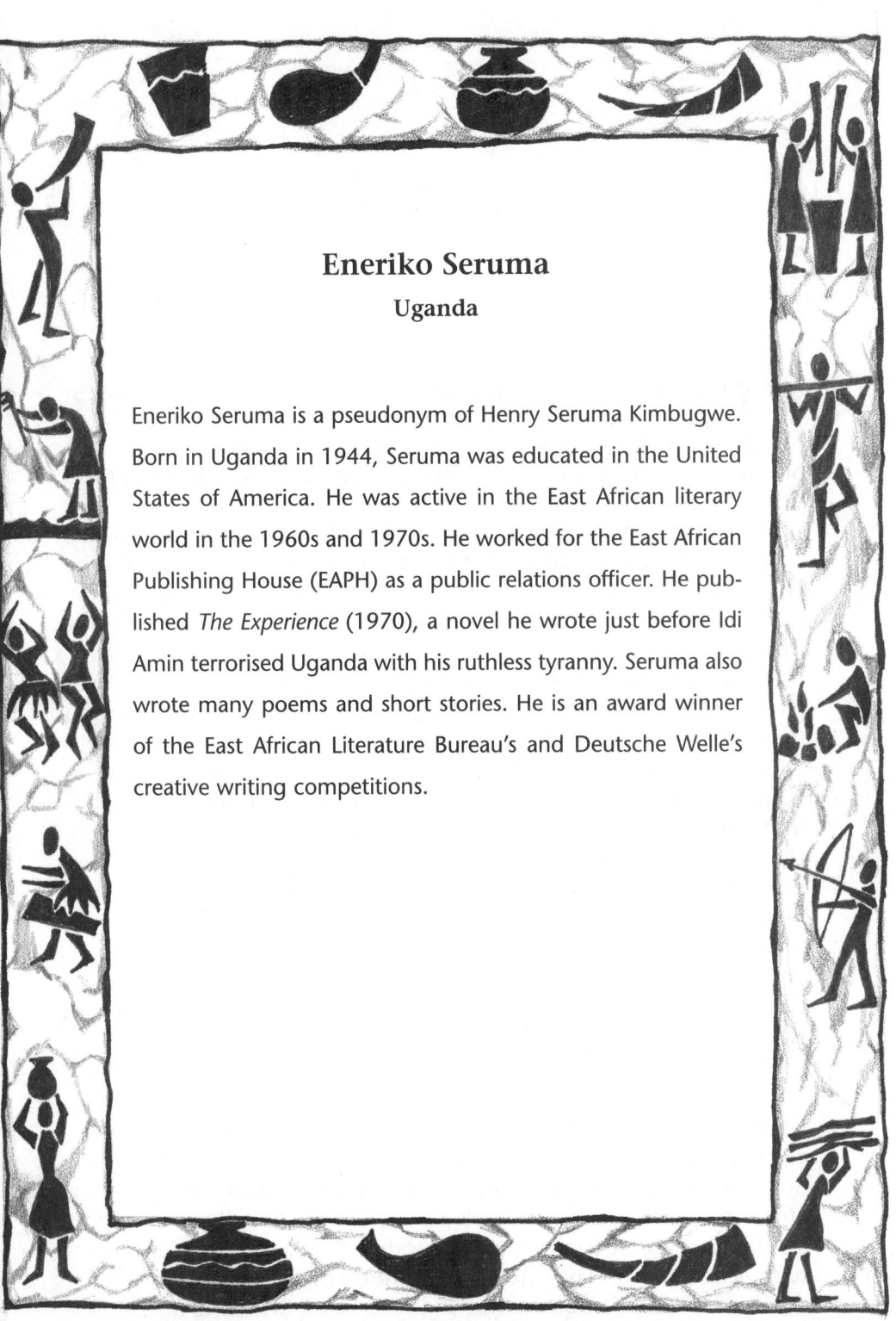

Eneriko Seruma
Uganda

Eneriko Seruma is a pseudonym of Henry Seruma Kimbugwe. Born in Uganda in 1944, Seruma was educated in the United States of America. He was active in the East African literary world in the 1960s and 1970s. He worked for the East African Publishing House (EAPH) as a public relations officer. He published *The Experience* (1970), a novel he wrote just before Idi Amin terrorised Uganda with his ruthless tyranny. Seruma also wrote many poems and short stories. He is an award winner of the East African Literature Bureau's and Deutsche Welle's creative writing competitions.

The Town

'The park is too crowded today. I wish I could afford to stay in bed on Saturdays,' the taxi driver said as he stopped the car in the Nakivubo car park, his eyes wandering over the crowd. 'But of course the more crowded it is, the more money there is to be earned,' he added, laughing to himself.

None of his passengers said anything; he had had a quiet load this run. His caller started calling out for new passengers in a quick, hoarse voice. 'Passengers for Wandegeya, Makerere, Bwaise, Kawempe; this way please. Makerere, Wandegeya …' His voice faded as he moved among the crowd.

The passengers got out of the cab, handing the fare to the driver. Each passenger, except the last one, disappeared into the crowd as soon as the change was handed back. The last passenger, a man who was a villager, stood some feet away from the car and watched the distant caller. 'And they like the town!' he thought. 'Instead of owning a small place in the village and farming for a better living, look at what they do. How can a man spend all day barking like a crazy dog?' He wondered how much the caller earned and walked over to the driver who was sitting in his car whistling to himself as he waited for passengers.

'How much does the caller earn?' he asked the driver.

'Fifty cents per car load. That's some money, you know. About eight, nine, maybe even ten shillings a day. And that's earned without any labouring too.'

The man thanked the driver and moved away. 'Yes,' he thought, 'that's the trouble with town people: they are always afraid of manual labour. They don't realise that because I dig from sunrise to midday I can sell five to six bags of coffee for a lot of money, and save because I don't have to buy food like they do. They spend all their money buying villagers' farm produce.' He took his eyes from the caller and walked away, squeezing among people of all sorts. 'What a gathering of characters!' he marvelled. 'They are all like vultures over a carcass.'

The man wished he could shut off the noise of the crowd; it was maddening. Not even at weddings and feasts – or even drinking parties – had he heard so much noise. Everybody seemed to be shouting; the noise seemed as if a cloud was hanging over the park and was striking him with bolts of noise.

'Here, miss, over here! I have the latest style ...'

'Over here, good lady! I have the latest fashion ...!'

'Natete! Natete! Passengers for Natete over here!'

'Here's a real nice cab. Over here, passengers, quick! It is comfortable; it has a radio; listen to your favourite songs as you go to Nakulabye.'

'This one is faster. You'll be there in a few minutes.'

'That is how they kill themselves,' the villager thought, 'driving fast as if bees were chasing them! Like that driver who brought me, how fast he had been driving – with one hand! One is safer in buses these days.' The man concluded his thoughts about the fast cars as other shouts hit his exhausted ears.

'Handkerchiefs! Handkerchiefs! Only forty cents, two for eighty cents. From your shilling you will be left with twenty cents for peanuts and popcorn. Two handkerchiefs for ...'

'Here, my lords, here! Pure woollen trousers for only thirty-five shillings. Only thirty-five shillings – cheaper than in the Asian shops. Here my ...'

'Katwe, Kibuye, Najja. Passengers for Katwe, Kibuye. The bus has just left, so don't miss this chance of a faster arrival. Katwe ...'

The villager stood and stared in wonderment. 'This is too much to believe! Do these men wake up in the morning to tell their wives they are going to work? Look at them, all shouting their heads off. What a way to earn a living!' He shook his head at the men who rushed at him with yards of cloth on their arms. There were so many of them. 'How can they make money with such competition?'

He looked out in the distance. All he could see were heads that bobbed and mouths that shouted. Here and there were some unfortunate travellers caught in a competition between callers, who were each shouting the experience of the driver they were working for. The poor travellers stood between them with worried looks on their faces, like prisoners standing in court while the defender and the prosecutor battle over their fate. Some travellers, caught between cloth-sellers, were entangled in rolls of cloth as the sellers showed off the quality of the materials.

The man turned his head and looked at the road and the entrance to the park. There was a traffic jam of cabs as they turned off the main street to enter the park. Horns hooted from cars that were full of impatient bewildered people, who stared out of the windows just like the monkeys that stared at the man every morning he went digging. Some of the passengers got out of the cars and walked the rest of the way. Dwarfing the cabs, that were mostly the small cars the villager called tortoises but which the town people called Volkswagens, were the double-decker buses that had both decks full of people going to all corners of Kampala city. The bus depot was opposite the taxi park; the man could see people lining the platforms and others scrambling to get into buses.

'How man does produce!' the man wondered. 'What thousands and thousands of people! One would think that there are no people left in the homes.' His heart missed a beat as he saw a young man run beside a bus and jump on to it. 'The fool,' he thought, remembering the man he once saw who missed when he tried to jump and got run over by the bus. 'Why are town people always in haste?' he wondered. 'Is it because they are living and working with the white people who always hurry as if they are afraid they won't make it to the outhouse?'

'Hear you, all people, hear!' a voice interrupted the man's thoughts. 'This is your chance to buy this incredible medicine. If your wife is unfaithful, if you are troubled by spirits, if your children are always sick, if you are impotent, if girls don't fall for you, if you have constant headache, stomach ache, mumps, dizziness, if you want to pass your exams successfully – everything, ladies and gentlemen, anything you want to get rid of, this is the medicine. Buy this medicine, this rare *mumbwa*[1]*,* and everything will be better.'

The villager looked toward the clear, booming voice. 'That is some strong medicine' he thought to himself, 'curing all those ailments. I wonder if it is just another way for the town people to earn money, or whether it is true.' He walked over to where the medicine-seller was sitting on a leopard skin, with all kinds of assortments laid out in front of him. Everything that looked odd seemed to be there, from live things like an eagle, a hawk, a snake, a rabbit, and other little animals, to dead things like a hyena, an antelope and a jackal.

'Yes?' the medicine-seller was looking at him. He had bloodshot eyes that never seemed to blink.

'You were talking about a *mumbwa* ...'

'Yes, yes. Are you impotent?' the medicine-seller asked. 'Is your wife running away? Are you troubled by your in-laws? Or are you after your neighbour's wife? She will be yours tonight if you buy this *mumbwa*. And what's more, he won't do a thing about it. But perhaps you have spirits of your grandparents disagreeing with the way you are spending the family fortune, uh? Oh, I know! You would like to win over one of these white things clicking around the city, wouldn't you, huh?'

'No, sir. White girls are for students at Makerere, not for people like me. They don't know how to bend their backs to cultivate. How can I,

a farmer, have a wife who doesn't dig? No, all I wanted ... you see, sir, I've had a lot of trouble with burglars, I thought ...'

'Oh, yes, of course, yes, yes, my friend,' the medicine-seller said, without a smile. 'This is the medicine for your troubles. Buy this and you are rid of them. If they ever ...' the medicine-seller stopped suddenly and cocked his head to one side. Then he sprang up with surprising speed and started running. Everybody was running and shouting, except the villager, who stood there staring stupidly at the place where the medicine-seller had been sitting. 'What is happening?' he asked himself.

'Run, everyone, run! Tax!'

'Tax raid! Run everybody! It is the entire blasted police force!'

The villager started running. There were so many people, he kept bumping into fear-crazed people who seemed blind, unable to distinguish women from men. The noise cloud seemed to have burst into ear-splitting fragment that whistled shrilly and shouted and cried hysterically. Among the crowd the villager could see the khaki uniforms of the policemen as they spread their huge arms wide apart to stop the fleeing tax-defaulters.

The villager ran because he had not paid his annual tax yet. 'What lousy luck!' he thought as he jumped over abandoned spreads of merchandise. Of all days, the police had chosen to raid on this one, when he was in town! Back in the village he could always avoid the less experienced village chief and his helpers. But here, with white officers commanding the policemen, they came so swiftly and silently like a dark cloud engulfing the sun. One never knew what was happening until the whole park was surrounded by policemen. They surrounded the park first, and then brought in more truckloads of policemen armed with short, effective clubs.

Revision questions

1. In this story, Seruma uses a number of similes to contrast town life and country life e.g. '...driving fast as if bees were chasing them.'
    a) Pick out four other such similes and show what aspect of city life each brings out.
    b) Why do you think it is only the villager/the man who uses figurative language and not the town people?
    c) There is also use of direct translation e.g. 'How man does produce!' Find out more of such expressions and rewrite them in formal English. Who uses such expressions and why?
2. In their own way, the town people are quite content in their way of life. How is this demonstrated by:
    a) taxi operators
    b) the traders?

3 Why does the villager get interested in the medicine-seller?
4 In what one aspect of life does the villager find himself in the same boat as the town people?

Topics for discussion
1 Discuss the use of dialogue in this story. How does it make the story more lively?
2 There is a lot of humour in this story. Do you agree? If so, give examples.
3 How long do you imagine the actions in this story took? What does that tell you about a short story compared to a novel?

Glossary
1 *Mumbwa*: (Luganda) Clay and fine sand mixed with crushed medicinal leaves, shaped into small cylinders and dried. The mumbwa is grated into a little water and the mixture drunk to cure various kinds of ailments.

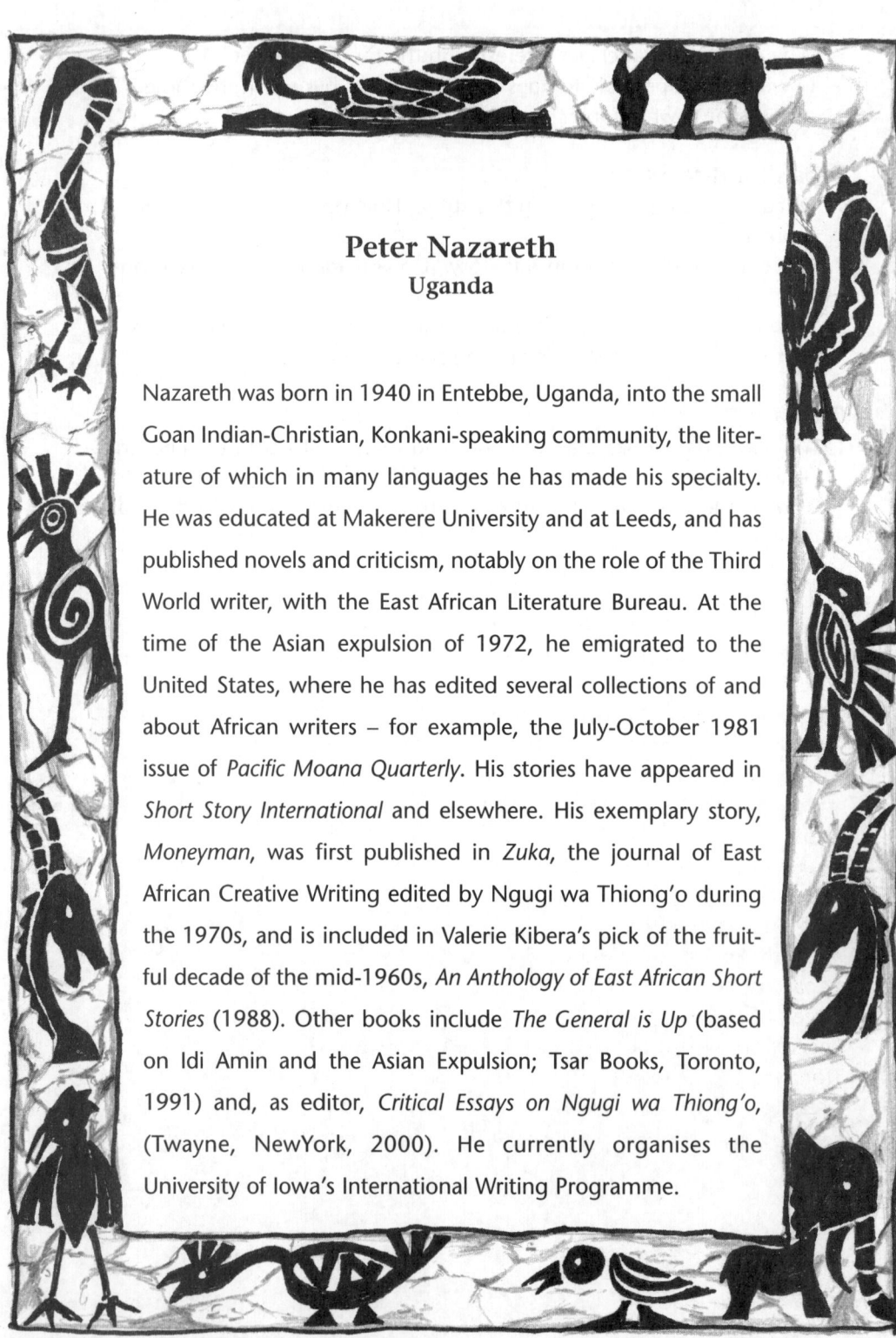

Peter Nazareth
Uganda

Nazareth was born in 1940 in Entebbe, Uganda, into the small Goan Indian-Christian, Konkani-speaking community, the literature of which in many languages he has made his specialty. He was educated at Makerere University and at Leeds, and has published novels and criticism, notably on the role of the Third World writer, with the East African Literature Bureau. At the time of the Asian expulsion of 1972, he emigrated to the United States, where he has edited several collections of and about African writers – for example, the July-October 1981 issue of *Pacific Moana Quarterly*. His stories have appeared in *Short Story International* and elsewhere. His exemplary story, *Moneyman*, was first published in *Zuka*, the journal of East African Creative Writing edited by Ngugi wa Thiong'o during the 1970s, and is included in Valerie Kibera's pick of the fruitful decade of the mid-1960s, *An Anthology of East African Short Stories* (1988). Other books include *The General is Up* (based on Idi Amin and the Asian Expulsion; Tsar Books, Toronto, 1991) and, as editor, *Critical Essays on Ngugi wa Thiong'o*, (Twayne, NewYork, 2000). He currently organises the University of Iowa's International Writing Programme.

Moneyman

Mr Manna Leitao had joined the civil service at a time when no Goans owned cars. In those days, it was quite normal for him to be seen walking all over the place, holding his umbrella like a walking-stick. But now, decades later, when Goans had passed through the bicycle age and were affluent enough to own cars, it was strange to see him drifting doggedly along the footpaths and bylanes. He seemed to creep along the edge of one's consciousness, until one suddenly wondered, 'Who is this odd-looking fellow?'

Odd-looking indeed he was. He had a large mouldy face. The hair on his head looked like one of those ferns you see at a swamp – pokers sticking out at the edges and disappearing into a disc at the centre. His ears italicised his head, hairs standing out of them like mini-television antennae. His lips looked sensual, lending credence to the story that he was secretly a satyr, although he had never married. The Goans thought that he had remained single because looking after a wife and children would cost too much.

He often boasted that he was the richest man in the little town of Apana. Incredible, for how could a lowly civil servant who never played the stock market get rich? Well, in two ways. The first was the straightforward one of usury. There were always other lowly civil servants in Apana, particularly Africans, who were dead broke around the third week of the month. The bankers never lent money to those who really needed it, so this was where The Man stepped in. He would lend money for a maximum period of two weeks at about forty per cent interest. Not per annum but per two weeks.

This is why Manna Leitao came to be known as Money Leitao and, finally, Moneyman.

Then there was the second way he made money. He did not spend any.

Late one evening, Mrs Carmen Dias heard a groaning outside her house. She told her husband and son to investigate. They found Moneyman lying in a gutter in their compound, holding his leg in

agony. The story went round later that Moneyman was chasing a spry young African miss across the lawns when he fell into the gutter and broke his leg. Yes, he broke his leg, as the Diases discovered eventually. They would have discovered it sooner had they taken him to the Grade A hospital but, despite his pain, he insisted that they take him to Grade B, where the poor were treated free of charge. His leg was put in plaster, and he was put to bed.

The Diases wrote about Moneyman's plight to his only traceable relatives, who lived in a neighbouring country. They arrived post-haste. Moneyman refused to see them. 'They have come here hoping I will die,' he said. 'They only want to get my money. Well, I won't, and they won't. Off with them!' Despite all efforts, the relatives had to give up and return home in disgust.

So Moneyman had to be looked after by the Diases. They felt that he was their responsibility as they had found him on their doorstep, so to speak. Who would look after this stubborn old man if they refused? They even cooked his meals because he said he could not eat African food. Father and son had to take turns cooking the meals because Mrs Dias had already made plans to go to Goa to visit her parents, and Moneyman's leg took a long time to heal. Needless to say, Moneyman did not pay the Diases anything, taking advantage of traditional Goan hospitality. What is more, after he realised that he was assured of regular meals, he started telling father and son what sort of meals to cook!

Moneyman's brush with death must have made him realise what a lonely man a single man is. At any rate, not long after he left the hospital, he gave up his lonely house and moved in with a family, the Fernandeses. The Fernandeses consisted of mother, father and three sons. It was surprising that they should take him in at all. Mother was a hard-headed, tough-hearted woman. Her husband, who owned a printing shop, was an inveterate drunkard and the eldest son was a playboy. The second son was taciturn and determined. Nobody knew what he was determined about, but it looked as though he had secret ambitions. The youngest son was kind-hearted, but he was painfully shy and it was difficult to imagine him breaking out of his shell and making contact with anybody.

Gradually it was noticed in Apana that Mrs Fernandes was running the printing shop. Mr Fernandes could be seen hanging around, cast aside like an empty bottle of liquor. The creditors had been about to foreclose when Mrs Fernandes stepped in. She paid off some of the debts and promised to pay the others in due course. The creditors agreed to wait provided she undertook to run the business herself. She accepted, even though she did not know anything about printing.

One day Moneyman turned up at the house of Mr Pobras D'Mello, one of the elders of the Apana Goan community. Mr D'Mello was puzzled to see him because Moneyman was not a social man, let alone a sociable one. After the formality of informal talk and drinks, Moneyman said, 'I would like your advice, Mr D'Mello.'

Surprised at this request, and secretly a little pleased, Mr D'Mello replied, 'Of course.'

'Please read this letter,' said Moneyman, handing over a sheet of paper.

'Mrs Fernandes,' read Mr D'Mello, 'you have abused my sympathy and my kind nature ...' and a few rude words followed. 'When you borrowed four thousand shillings from me in June, you promised to repay it, plus a small lending charge, within three months. But you have not paid anything, and I demand it all back immediately you ...' and a few obscenities followed.

'Well?' said Moneyman.

'Well?' said Mr D'Mello.

'Don't you think it is a good letter?' said Moneyman.

Mr D'Mello was known for his tact, so instead of answering directly he said, 'Tell me a little more about this matter.'

'Mrs Fernandes was in trouble because of her husband's debts. She begged me to do her a favour and lend her four thousand shillings to pay off the debts. Feeling sorry, I lent her the money. Besides, I had already stood guarantee for her son's purchase of petrol, and the other day I had to pay a bill of nine hundred shillings ...'

'You mention a service charge in your letter,' said Mr D'Mello. 'What is this?'

'Well, you know,' said Moneyman. 'I lost interest by drawing my money from my savings account at the bank, so it is but fair that I should be compensated ...'

'How much?' said Mr D'Mello.

'I ... er ... er,' said Moneyman.

'How much?' said Mr D'Mello, a little sharply. 'How much is the service charge?'

'Er ... one ... two thousand shillings ...'

'Per annum?' asked Mr D'Mello, amazed.

'No, to be paid as soon as the money was due.'

'Well, do you want to know what I think?' said Mr D'Mello. 'I think you are a mean, miserable skinflint. However, you have asked for my advice in respect of this ... this letter, and I shall give it. The letter is extremely rude and offensive and, if you send it, Mrs Fernandes can use it to take legal action against you. Besides, from what you say, I don't think you have it in writing that you gave her the loan – '

'I already gave her the letter this morning,' said Moneyman.

'Then I will ask you to kindly leave my house,' said Mr D'Mello.

Moneyman got back home in time for dinner. He sat at the dinner table, where the atmosphere was decidedly frosty. Finally, he said in Konkani, '*Udoi coddi*,' which should mean 'pass the curry' but, if translated literally, means 'throw the curry'. And the second son did just that. He picked up the dish of curry and threw it at Moneyman.

'You bastard,' he yelled at him. 'You have been staying with us, no? Do the few shillings you have lent us make up for the inconvenience? But you have the cheek to write an insulting letter to my mother! I'll teach you!' And he began beating up the old man.

The eldest and the youngest sons pulled the second son back, but not before Moneyman had had his other leg broken. The eldest son had to take him to the Grade B hospital. After all, the car contained Moneyman's petrol.

Moneyman was abandoned at Grade B. He sent word to the Diases, who found this time that they could leave a stubborn old man to his distress without any qualms of conscience. When Moneyman was finally discharged, he did not press charges. He had nothing in writing, while the Fernandeses had. Besides, the lawyer would cost too much.

But Manna Leitao has benefited from his experience; he has learnt his lesson. He does not trust people any more; people are not as dependable as money. He can still be seen walking around Apana, shabbily dressed and with his ubiquitous umbrella; and whenever he passes the thriving Fernandes Press, he mutters to himself and tightens his grip on his umbrella, as though it is a bankroll from which he does not wish to be parted.

Revision questions

1. a) How did Mr Manna Leitao come to be called Moneyman?
   b) Do you find any relationship between his names – Manna and Moneyman - and his character?
2. a) How did Moneyman get rich?
   b) Would you encourage people to get rich that way?
3. a) What is usury? Do you know people who practise it?
   b) Are usurers respected people in society?
4. 'Mr Moneyman's miserliness bordered on the comical'. Explain this statement using three distinct examples from the story.
5. a) Describe each of the members of the Fernandes' family.
   b) Why do you think it was surprising that they took Moneyman into their home?
6. What is your assessment of Mr Pobras D'Mello?
7. Would you describe Moneyman as an eccentric character? Why or why not?

8 Pick out four examples of the use of similes in this story and show how each is used to make the descriptions lively.

Topics for discussion
1 There is a good attempt to develop most of the characters in this story. Discuss and show how this is done.
2 It is said every dog has its day.
    a) How does this apply to Moneyman?
    b) How did Moneyman meet his match in:
       i) Mr Pobras D'Mello
       ii) The Fernandes' second son?
3 a) What lessons did Moneyman learn when he got injured the second time?
    b) What lesson do you learn from this story?
    c) Suggest ways in which you think misers can be helped.

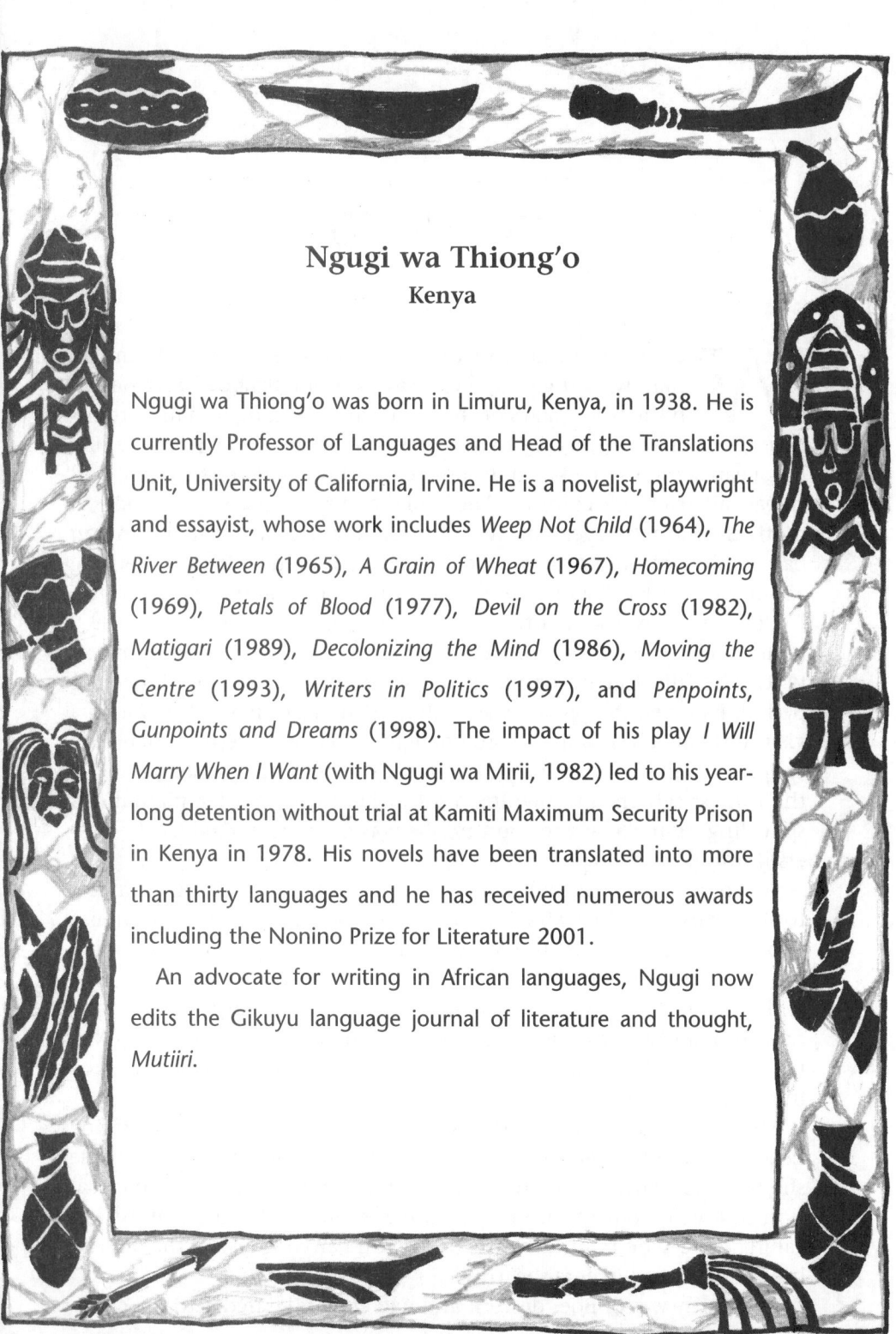

Ngugi wa Thiong'o
Kenya

Ngugi wa Thiong'o was born in Limuru, Kenya, in 1938. He is currently Professor of Languages and Head of the Translations Unit, University of California, Irvine. He is a novelist, playwright and essayist, whose work includes *Weep Not Child* (1964), *The River Between* (1965), *A Grain of Wheat* (1967), *Homecoming* (1969), *Petals of Blood* (1977), *Devil on the Cross* (1982), *Matigari* (1989), *Decolonizing the Mind* (1986), *Moving the Centre* (1993), *Writers in Politics* (1997), and *Penpoints, Gunpoints and Dreams* (1998). The impact of his play *I Will Marry When I Want* (with Ngugi wa Mirii, 1982) led to his year-long detention without trial at Kamiti Maximum Security Prison in Kenya in 1978. His novels have been translated into more than thirty languages and he has received numerous awards including the Nonino Prize for Literature 2001.

An advocate for writing in African languages, Ngugi now edits the Gikuyu language journal of literature and thought, *Mutiiri*.

The Martyr

When Mr and Mrs Garstone were murdered in their home by unknown gangsters, there was a lot of talk about it. It was all on the front pages of the daily papers and figured importantly in the Radio Newsreel. Perhaps this was so because they were the first European settlers to be killed in the increased wave of violence that had spread all over the country. The violence was said to have political motives. And wherever you went, in the marketplaces, in the Indian bazaars, in a remote African *duka*, you were bound to hear something about the murder. There were a variety of accounts and interpretations.

Nowhere was the matter more thoroughly discussed than in a remote, lonely house built on a hill, which belonged, quite appropriately, to Mrs Hill. Her husband, an old veteran settler of the pioneering period, had died the previous year after an attack of malaria while on a visit to Uganda. Her only son and daughter were now getting their education at 'Home' – home being another name for England. Being one of the earliest settlers and owning a lot of land with big tea plantations sprawling right across the country, she was much respected by the others if not liked by all.

For some did not like what they considered her too 'liberal' attitudes to the 'natives'. When Mrs Smiles and Mrs Hardy came into her house two days later to discuss the murder, they wore a look of sad triumph – sad because Europeans (not just Mr and Mrs Garstone) had been killed, and of triumph, because the essential depravity and ingratitude of the natives had been demonstrated beyond all doubt. No longer could Mrs Hill maintain that natives could be civilised if only they were handled in the right manner.

Mrs Smiles was a lean, middle-aged woman whose tough, determined nose and tight lips reminded one so vividly of a missionary. In a sense she was. Convinced that she and her kind formed an oasis of civilisation in a wild country of savage people, she considered it almost her calling to keep on reminding the natives and anyone else of the fact, by her gait, talk and general bearing.

Mrs Hardy was of Boer descent and had early migrated into the country from South Africa. Having no opinions of her own about anything, she mostly found herself agreeing with any views that most approximated those of her husband and her race. For instance, on this day she found herself in agreement with whatever Mrs Smiles said. Mrs Hill stuck to her guns and maintained, as indeed she had always done, that the natives were obedient at heart and all you needed was to treat them kindly.

'That's all they need. Treat them kindly. They will talk kindly to you. Look at my "boys". They all love me. They would do anything I ask them to!' That was her philosophy and it was shared by quite a number of the liberal, progressive type. Mrs Hill had done some liberal things for her 'boys'. Not only had she built some brick quarters (brick, mind you) but had also put up a school for the children. It did not matter if the school had not enough teachers or if the children learnt only half a day and worked in the plantations for the other half; it was more than most other settlers had the courage to do!

'It is horrible. Oh, a horrible act,' declared Mrs Smiles rather vehemently. Mrs Hardy agreed. Mrs Hill remained neutral.

'How could they do it? We've brought 'em civilisation. We've stopped slavery and tribal wars. Were they not all leading savage miserable lives?' Mrs Smiles spoke with all her powers of oratory. Then she concluded with a sad shake of the head: 'But I've always said they'll never be civilised, simply can't take it.'

'We should show tolerance,' suggested Mrs Hill. Her tone spoke more of the missionary than Mrs Smiles's looks.

'Tolerant! Tolerant! How long shall we continue being tolerant? Who could have been more tolerant than the Garstones? Who more kind? And to think of all the squatters they maintained!'

'Well, it isn't the squatters who ...'

'Who did? Who did?'

'They should all be hanged!' suggested Mrs Hardy. There was conviction in her voice.

'And to think they were actually called from bed by their houseboy!'

'Indeed?'

'Yes. It was their houseboy who knocked at their door and urgently asked them to open. Said some people were after him – '

'Perhaps there – '

'No! It was all planned. All a trick. As soon as the door was opened, the gang rushed in. It's all in the paper.'

Mrs Hill looked away rather guiltily. She had not read her paper.

It was time for tea. She excused herself and went near the door and called out in a kind, shrill voice.

'Njoroge! Njoroge!'

Njoroge was her 'houseboy'. He was a tall, broad-shouldered man nearing middle age. He had been in the Hills' service for more than ten years. He wore green trousers, with a red cloth-band round the waist and a red fez on his head. He now appeared at the door and raised his eyebrows in inquiry – an action which with him accompanied the words, 'Yes Memsahib?' or '*Ndio, bwana.*'

'*Leta chai.*'

'*Ndio*, Memsahib!' and he vanished back after casting a quick glance round all the memsahibs there assembled. The conversation which had been interrupted by Njoroge's appearance was now resumed.

'They look so innocent,' said Mrs Hardy.

'Yes. Quite the innocent flower but the serpent under it.' Mrs Smiles was acquainted with Shakespeare.

'Been with me for ten years or so. Very faithful. Likes me very much.' Mrs Hill was defending her 'boy'.

'All the same I don't like him. I don't like his face.'

'The same with me.'

Tea was brought. They drank, still chatting about the death, the government's policy, and the political demagogues who were undesirable elements in this otherwise beautiful country. But Mrs Hill maintained that these semi-illiterate demagogues who went to Britain and thought they had education did not know the true aspirations of their people. You could still win your 'boys' by being kind to them.

Nevertheless, when Mrs Smiles and Mrs Hardy had gone, she brooded over that murder and the conversation. She felt uneasy and for the first time noticed that she lived a bit too far from any help in case of an attack. The knowledge that she had a pistol was a comfort.

Supper was over. That ended Njoroge's day. He stepped out of the light into the countless shadows and then vanished into the darkness. He was following the footpath from Mrs Hill's house to the workers' quarters down the hill. He tried to whistle to dispel the silence and loneliness that hung around him. He could not. Instead he heard a bird cry, sharp, shrill. Strange thing for a bird to cry at night.

He stopped, stood stock-still. Below, he could perceive nothing. But behind him the immense silhouette of Memsahib's house – large, imposing – could be seen. He looked back intently, angrily. In his anger, he suddenly thought he was growing old.

'You. You. I've lived with you so long. And you've reduced me to this!' Njoroge wanted to shout to the house all this and many other things that had long accumulated in his heart. The house would not respond. He felt foolish and moved on.

Again the bird cried. Twice!

'A warning to her,' Njoroge thought. And again his whole soul rose in anger – anger against those with a white skin, those foreign elements that had displaced the true sons of the land from their God-given place. Had God not promised Gekoyo all this land, he and his children, forever and ever? Now the land had been taken away.

He remembered his father, as he always did when these moments of anger and bitterness possessed him. He had died in the struggle – the struggle to rebuild the destroyed shrines. That was at the famous 1923 Nairobi Massacre when police fired on a people peacefully demonstrating for their rights. His father was among the people who died. Since then Njoroge had had to struggle for a living – seeking employment here and there on European farms. He had met many types – some harsh, some kind, but all dominating, giving him just what salary they thought fit for him. Then he had come to be employed by the Hills. It was a strange coincidence that he had come here. A big portion of the land now occupied by Mrs Hill was the land his father had shown him as belonging to the family. They had found the land occupied when his father and some of the others had temporarily retired to Muranga owing to famine. They had come back and *Ng'o* ! the land was gone.

'Do you see that fig tree? Remember that land is yours. Be patient. Watch these Europeans. They will go and then you can claim the land.'

He was small then. After his father's death, Njoroge had forgotten this injunction. But when he coincidentally came here and saw the tree, he remembered. He knew it all – all by heart. He knew where every boundary went through.

Njoroge had never liked Mrs Hill. He had always resented her complacency in thinking she had done so much for the workers. He had worked with cruel types like Mrs Smiles and Mrs Hardy. But he always knew where he stood with such. But Mrs Hill! Her liberalism was almost smothering. Njoroge hated settlers. He hated above all what he thought was their hypocrisy and complacency. He knew that Mrs Hill was no exception. She was like all the others, only she loved paternalism. It convinced her she was better than the others. But she was worse. You did not know exactly where you stood with her.

All of a sudden, Njoroge shouted, 'I hate them! I hate them!' Then a grim satisfaction came over him. Tonight, anyway, Mrs Hill would die – pay for her own smug liberalism, her paternalism and pay for all the sins of her settler race. It would be one settler less.

He came to his own room. There was no smoke coming from all the other rooms belonging to the other workers. The lights had even gone out in many of them. Perhaps, some were already asleep or gone to the Native Reserve to drink beer. He lit the lantern and sat on the bed. It was a very small room. Sitting on the bed one could almost touch all the corners of the room if one stretched one's arms wide. Yet it was here,

here, that he with two wives and a number of children had to live, had in fact lived for more than five years. So crammed! Yet Mrs Hill thought that she had done enough by just having the houses built with brick.

'*Mzuri sana*, eh?' (very good, eh?) she was very fond of asking. And whenever she had visitors she brought them to the edge of the hill and pointed at the houses.

Again Njoroge smiled grimly to think how Mrs Hill would pay for all this self-congratulatory piety. He also knew that he had an axe to grind. He had to avenge the death of his father and strike a blow for the occupied family land. It was foresight on his part to have taken his wives and children back to the Reserve. They might else have been in the way and in any case he did not want to bring trouble to them should he be forced to run away after the act.

The other *Ihii* ('Freedom Boys') would come at any time now. He would lead them to the house. Treacherous – yes! But how necessary.

The cry of the night bird, this time louder than ever, reached his ears. That was a bad omen. It always portended death – death for Mrs Hill. He thought of her. He remembered her. He had lived with Memsahib and *Bwana* for more than ten years. He knew that she had loved her husband. Of that he was sure. She almost died of grief when she had learnt of his death. In that moment her settlerism had been shorn off. In that naked moment, Njoroge had been able to pity her. Then the children! He had known them. He had seen them grow up like any other children. Almost like his own. They loved their parents, and Mrs Hill had always been so tender with them, so loving. He thought of them in England, wherever that was, fatherless and motherless.

And then he realised, too suddenly, that he could not do it. He could not tell how, but Mrs Hill had suddenly crystallised into a woman, a wife, somebody like Njeri or Wambui, and above all, a mother. He could not kill a woman. He could not kill a mother. He hated himself for this change. He felt agitated. He tried hard to put himself in the other condition, his former self and see her as just a settler. As a settler, it was easy. For Njoroge hated settlers and all Europeans. If only he could see her like this (as one among many white men or settlers) then he could do it. Without scruples. But he could not bring back the other self. Not now, anyway. He had never thought of her in these terms. Until today. And yet he knew she was the same, and would be the same tomorrow – a patronising, complacent woman. It was then that he knew he was a divided man and perhaps would ever remain like that. For now it even seemed an impossible thing to snap just like that ten years of relationship, though to him they had been years of pain and shame. He prayed and wished there had never been injustices. Then there would never have been this rift – the rift between white and black. Then he would never have been put in this painful situation.

What was he to do now? Would he betray the 'Boys'? He sat there, irresolute, unable to decide on a course of action. If only he had not thought of her in human terms! That he hated settlers was quite clear in his mind. But to kill a mother of two seemed too painful a task for him to do in a free frame of mind.

He went out.

Darkness still covered him and he could see nothing clearly. The stars above seemed to be anxiously waiting Njoroge's decision. Then, as if their cold stare was compelling him, he began to walk, walk back to Mrs Hill's house. He had decided to save her. Then probably he would go to the forest. There, he would forever fight with a freer conscience. That seemed excellent. It would also serve as a propitiation for his betrayal of the other 'Boys'.

There was no time to lose. It was already late and the 'Boys' might come any time. So he ran with one purpose – to save the woman. At the road he heard footsteps. He stepped into the bush and lay still. He was certain that those were the 'Boys'. He waited breathlessly for the footsteps to die. Again he hated himself for this betrayal. But how could he fail to hearken to this other voice? He ran on when the footsteps had died. It was necessary to run, for if the 'Boys' discovered his betrayal he would surely meet death. But then he did not mind this. He only wanted to finish this other task first.

At last, sweating and panting, he reached Mrs Hill's house and knocked at the door, crying 'Memsahib! Memsahib!'

Mrs Hill had not yet gone to bed. She had sat up, a multitude of thoughts crossing her mind. Ever since that afternoon's conversation with the other women, she had felt more and more uneasy. When Njoroge went and she was left alone she had gone to her safe and taken out her pistol, with which she was now toying. It was better to be prepared. It was unfortunate that her husband had died. He might have kept her company.

She sighed over and over again as she remembered her pioneering days. She and her husband and others had tamed the wilderness of this country and had developed a whole mass of unoccupied land. People like Njoroge now lived contented without a single worry about tribal wars. They had a lot to thank the Europeans for.

Yes she did not like those politicians who came to corrupt the otherwise obedient and hard-working men, especially when treated kindly. She did not like this murder of the Garstones. No! She did not like it. And when she remembered the fact that she was really alone, she thought it might be better for her to move down to Nairobi or

The Martyr

Kinangop and stay with friends a while. But what would she do with her boys? Leave them there? She wondered. She thought of Njoroge. A queer boy. Had he many wives? Had he a large family? It was surprising even to her to find that she had lived with him so long, yet had never thought of these things. This reflection shocked her a little. It was the first time she had ever thought of him as a man with a family. She had always seen him as a servant. Even now it seemed ridiculous to think of her houseboy as a father with a family. She sighed. This was an omission, something to be righted in future.

And then she heard a knock on the front door and a voice calling out 'Memsahib! Memsahib!'

It was Njoroge's voice. Her houseboy. Sweat broke out on her face. She could not even hear what the boy was saying for the circumstances of the Garstones' death came to her. This was her end. The end of the road. So Njoroge had led them here! She trembled and felt weak.

But suddenly, strength came back to her. She knew she was alone. She knew they would break in. No! She would die bravely. Holding her pistol more firmly in her hand, she opened the door and quickly fired. Then a nausea came over her. She had killed a man for the first time. She felt weak and fell down crying, 'Come and kill me!' She did not know that she had in fact killed her saviour.

On the following day, it was all in the papers. That a single woman could fight a gang fifty strong was bravery unknown. And to think she had killed one too!

Mrs Smiles and Mrs Hardy were especially profuse in their congratulations.

'We told you they're all bad.'

'They are all bad,' agreed Mrs Hardy. Mrs Hill kept quiet. The circumstances of Njoroge's death worried her. The more she thought about it, the more of a puzzle it was to her. She gazed still into space. Then she let out a slow enigmatic sigh.

'I don't know,' she said.

'Don't know?' Mrs Hardy asked.

'Yes. That's it. Inscrutable.' Mrs Smiles was triumphant. 'All of them should be whipped.'

'All of them should be whipped,' agreed Mrs Hardy.

Revision questions

1 For what reason did Mrs Smiles and Mrs Hardy visit Mrs Hill?
2 Who were the natives and who were the settlers? How did the two groups relate to one another?
3 a) In what way did Mrs Hill's attitude towards Africans differ from that of Mrs Smiles and Mrs Hardy.

The Martyr

    b) How did the conversation between Mrs Hill and the other ladies affect her attitude towards her 'boys'?
4 Why did Njoroge have a special disliking towards the settlers?
5 "Would he betray the 'Boys'?" What had Mrs Hill's workers planned to do?
6 a) Why did Njoroge change his mind about killing Mrs Hill? What does this tell you about his character?
    b) There is a good attempt in this story to develop the characters. Write notes on the characters of:
       i) Mrs Hill
       ii) Njoroge
       iii) Mrs Smiles
       iv) Njoroge's father.
7 Ngugi tells his story in quite a controlled way but intrudes to comment on or satirise the characters. How is this done in respect to:
    a) Mrs Hill
    b) Njoroge?
8 What do you think the night cry of the bird portends?

Topics for discussion
1 This story is about the colonial era and the struggle for independence in Kenya. From the story, what do you think led to the struggle?
2 What is a flashback? How does the use of flashbacks in this story help us appreciate what happens in the short time the actions in this story take place?
3 Ngugi uses vivid descriptions to bring out his characters' thoughts, motives and desires which helps the reader understand the characters better. How is this true of Mrs Hill and Njoroge?
4 Who is a martyr? In what way is Njoroge the martyr in this story?

A Meeting in the Dark

He stood at the door of the hut and saw his old, frail but energetic father coming along the village street, with a rather dirty bag made out of a strong *calico* swinging by his side. His father always carried this bag. John knew what it contained: a Bible, a hymn-book and probably a notebook and a pen. His father was a preacher. He knew it was he who had stopped his mother from telling him stories when he became a man of God. His mother had stopped telling him stories long ago. She would say to him, 'Now, don't ask for any more stories. Your father may come.' So he feared his father. John went in and warned his mother of his father's coming. Then his father entered. John stood aside, then walked towards the door. He lingered there doubtfully, then he went out.

'John, *hei*, John!'

'*Baba!*'

'Come back.'

He stood doubtfully in front of his father. His heart beat faster and there was that anxious voice within him asking: Does he know?

'Sit down. Where are you going?'

'For a walk, Father,' he answered evasively.

'To the village?'

'Well-yes-no. I mean, nowhere in particular.' John saw his father look at him hard, seeming to read his face. John sighed, a very slow sigh. He did not like the way his father eyed him. He always looked at him as though John was a sinner, one who had to be watched all the time. 'I am,' his heart told him. John guiltily refused to meet the old man's gaze and looked past him appealingly to his mother who was quietly peeling potatoes. But she seemed oblivious of everything around her.

'Why do you look away? What have you done?'

John shrank within himself with fear. But his face remained expressionless. He could hear the loud beats of his heart. It was like an engine pumping water. He felt no doubt his father knew all about it. He thought: 'Why does he torture me: why does he not at once say he knows?' Then another voice told him: 'No, he doesn't know, otherwise he would have already jumped at you.' A consolation. He faced his thoughtful father with courage.

'When is the journey?'

Again John thought: Why does he ask? I have told him many times.

'Next week, Tuesday,' he said.

'Right. Tomorrow we go to the shops, hear?'

'Yes, Father.'

'Then be prepared.'

'Yes, Father.'

'You can go.'

'Thank you, Father.' He began to move.

'John!'

'Yes?' John's heart almost stopped beating.

'You seem to be in a hurry. I don't want to hear of you loitering in the village. I know young men, going to show off just because you are going away? I don't want to hear of trouble in the village.'

Much relieved, he went out. He could guess what his father meant by not wanting trouble in the village.

'Why do you persecute the boy so much?' Susana spoke for the first time. Apparently she had carefully listened to the whole drama without a word. Now was her time to speak. She looked at her tough old preacher who had been a companion for life. She had married him a long time ago. She could not tell the number of years. They had been happy. Then the man became a convert. And everything in the home put on a religious tone. He even made her stop telling stories to the child. 'Tell him of Jesus. Jesus died for you. Jesus died for the child. He must know the Lord.' She, too, had been converted. But she was never blind to the moral torture he inflicted on the boy (that was how she always referred to John), so that the boy had grown up mortally afraid of his father. She always wondered if it was love for the son. Or could it be a resentment because, well, they too had 'sinned' before marriage? John had been the result of that sin. But that had not been John's fault. It was the boy who ought to complain. She often wondered if the boy had ... but no. The boy had been very small when they left Fort Hall. She looked at her husband. He remained mute though his left hand did, rather irritably, feel about his face.

'It is as if he was not your son. Or do you ...'

'Hm, Sister.' The voice was pleading. She was seeking a quarrel but he did not feel equal to one. Really, women could never understand. Women were women, whether saved or not. Their son had to be protected against all evil influences. He must be made to grow in the footsteps of the Lord. He looked at her, frowning a little. She had made him sin but that had been a long time ago. And he had been saved. John must not tread the same road.

'You ought to tell us to leave. You know I can go away. Go back to Fort Hall. And then everybody ...'

'Look, Sister,' he hastily interrupted. He always called her sister. Sister-in-Lord, in full. But he sometimes wondered if she had been truly saved. In his heart he prayed: Lord, be with our sister Susana. Aloud, he continued, 'You know I want the boy to grow in the Lord.'

'But you torture him so! You make him fear you!'

'Why! He should not fear me. I have really nothing against him.'

'It is you. You. You have always been cruel to him ...' She stood up. The peelings dropped from her frock and fell in a heap on the floor. 'Stanley!'

'Sister.' He was startled by the vehemence in her voice. He had never seen her like this. Lord, take the devil out of her. Save her this minute. She did not say what she wanted to say. Stanley looked away from her. It was a surprise, but it seemed he feared his wife. If you had told the people in the village about this, they would not have believed you. He took his Bible and began to read. On Sunday he would preach to a congregation of brethren and sisters.

Susana, a rather tall, thin woman, who had once been beautiful, sat down again and went on with her work. She did not know what was troubling her son. Was it the coming journey? Still, she feared for him.

Outside, John was strolling aimlessly along the path that led from his home. He stood near the wattle tree which was a little way from his father's house and surveyed the whole village. They lay before his eyes, crammed, rows and rows of mud and grass huts, ending in sharply defined sticks that pointed to heaven. Smoke was coming out of various huts. It was an indication that many women had already come from the shambas. Night would soon fall. To the west, the sun – that lone daytime traveller – was hurrying home behind the misty hills. Again, John looked at the crammed rows and rows of huts that formed Makeno Village, one of the new mushroom 'towns' that grew up all over the country during the Mau Mau war. It looked so ugly. A pain rose in his heart and he felt like crying – I hate you, I hate you! You trapped me alive. Away from you, it would never have happened. He did not shout. He just watched.

A woman was coming towards where he stood. A path into the village was just near there. She was carrying a big load of *kuni* which bent her into an Akamba-bow shape. She greeted him. 'Is it well with you, *Njooni* (John)?'

'It is well with me, Mother.' There was no trace of bitterness in his voice. John was by nature polite. Everyone knew this. He was quite unlike the other proud, educated sons of the tribe – sons who came back from the other side of the waters with white or Negro wives who spoke English. And they behaved just like Europeans! John was a favourite, a model of humility and moral perfection. Everyone knew that though a clergyman's son, John would never betray the tribe. They still talked of the tribe and its ways.

'When are you going to – to –'

'Makerere?'

'Makelele.' She laughed. The way she pronounced the name was funny. And the way she laughed, too. She enjoyed it. But John felt hurt. So everyone knew of this.

'Next week.'

'I wish you well.'

'Thank you, Mother.'

She said quietly, as if trying to pronounce it better 'Makelele'. She laughed at herself again but she was tired. The load was heavy.

'Stay well, Son.'

'Go well and in peace, Mother.'

And the woman who all the time had stood, moved on, panting like a donkey, but she was obviously pleased with John's politeness.

John remained long, looking at her. What made such a woman live on day to day, working hard, yet happy? Had she much faith in life? Or was her faith in the tribe? She and her kind, who had never been touched by ways of the whiteman, looked as though they had something to cling to. As he watched her disappear, he felt proud that they should think well of him. He felt proud that he had a place in their esteem. And then came the pang. Father will know. They will know. He did not know what he feared most; the action his father would take when he found out, or the loss of the little faith the simple villagers had placed in him, when they knew. He feared to lose everything.

He went down to the small local tea-shop. He met many people who wished him well at the college. All of them knew that the priest's son had finished all the whiteman's learning in Kenya. He would now go to Uganda. They had read this in the *Baraza*, the Swahili weekly. John did not stay long at the shop. The sun had already gone to rest and now darkness was coming. The evening meal was ready. His tough father was still at the table reading his Bible. He did not look up when John entered. Strange silence settled in the hut.

'You look unhappy.' His mother first broke the silence.

John laughed. It was a nervous little laugh. 'No, Mother,' he hastily replied, nervously looking at his father. He secretly hoped that Wamuhu had not blabbed.

'Then I am glad.'

She did not know. He ate his dinner and went out to his hut. A man's hut. Every young man had his own hut. John was never allowed to bring any girl visitor in there. Stanley did not want 'trouble'. Even to be seen standing with one was a crime. His father could easily thrash him. He feared his father, though sometimes he wondered why he feared him. He ought to have rebelled like the other educated young men. He lit the lantern. He took it in his hand. The yellow light flickered dangerously and then went out. He knew his hands were shaking. He lit it again and hurriedly took his big coat and a huge *kofia* which were lying on the unmade bed. He left the lantern burning, so that his father would see it and think he was in. John bit his lower lip spitefully. He hated himself for being so girlish. It was unnatural for a boy of his age.

Like a shadow, he stealthily crossed the courtyard and went on to the village street.

He met young men and women lining the streets. They were laughing, talking, whispering. They were obviously enjoying themselves. John thought, they are freer than I am. He envied their exuberance. They clearly stood outside or above the strict morality that the educated ones had to be judged by. Would he have gladly changed places with them? He wondered. At last, he came to the hut. It stood at the very heart of the village. How well he knew it – to his sorrow. He wondered what he should do! Wait for her outside? What if her mother came out instead? He decided to enter.

'*Hodi!*'

'Enter. We are in.'

John pulled down his hat before he entered. Indeed they were all there – all except she whom he wanted. The fire in the hearth was dying. Only a small flame from a lighted lantern vaguely illuminated the whole hut. The flame and the giant shadow created on the wall seemed to be mocking him. He prayed that Wamuhu's parents would not recognise him. He tried to be 'thin', and to disguise his voice as he greeted them. They recognised him and made themselves busy on his account. To be visited by such an educated one, who knew all about the whiteman's world and knowledge and who would now go to another land beyond, was not such a frequent occurrence that it could be taken lightly. Who knew but he might be interested in their daughter? Stranger things had happened. After all, learning was not the only thing. Though Wamuhu had no learning, yet she had charms and could be trusted to captivate any young man's heart with her looks and smiles.

'You will sit down. Take that stool.'

'No!' He noticed with bitterness that he did not call her 'Mother'.

Ngugi wa Thiong'o

'Where is Wamuhu?'

The mother threw a triumphant glance at her husband. They exchanged a knowing look. John bit his lip again and felt like bolting. He controlled himself with difficulty.

'She has gone out to get some tea leaves. Please sit down. She will cook you some tea when she comes.'

'I am afraid ...' he muttered some inaudible words and went out. He almost collided with Wamuhu.

In the hut: 'Didn't I tell you? Trust a woman's eye!'

'You don't know these young men.'

'But you see John is different. Everyone speaks well of him and he is a clergyman's son.'

'Y-e-e-s! A clergyman's son! You forget your daughter is circumcised.' The old man was remembering his own day. He had found for himself a good virtuous woman, initiated in all the tribe's ways. And she had known no other man. He had married her. They were happy. Other men of his *Rika* had done the same. All the girls had been virgins, it being a taboo to touch a girl in that way, even if you slept in the same bed, as indeed so many young men and girls did. Then the white men had come, preaching a strange religion, strange ways, which all men followed. The tribe's code of behaviour was broken. The new faith could not keep the tribe together. How could it? The men who followed the new faith would not let the girls be circumcised. And they would not let their sons marry circumcised girls. *Puu*! Look at what was happening. Their young men went away to the land of the whitemen. What did they bring? White women. Black women who spoke English. Aaa – bad. And the young men who were left just did not mind. They made unmarried girls their wives and then left them with fatherless children.

'What does it matter?' his wife was replying. 'Is Wamuhu not as good as the best of them? Anyway, John is different.'

'Different! Different! *Puu*! They are all alike. Those coated with the white clay of the whiteman's ways are the worst. They have nothing inside. Nothing – nothing here.' He took a piece of wood and nervously poked the dying fire. A strange numbness came over him. He trembled. And he feared; he feared for the tribe. For now he saw it was not only the educated men who were coated with strange ways, but the whole tribe. The old man trembled and cried inside mourning for a tribe that had crumbled. The tribe had nowhere to go to. And it could not be what it was before. He stopped poking and looked hard at the ground.

'I wonder why he came. I wonder.' Then he looked at his wife and said, 'Have you seen strange behaviour with your daughter?'

His wife did not answer. She was preoccupied with her own great hopes.

John and Wamuhu walked on in silence. The intricate streets and turns were well known to them both. Wamuhu walked with quick light steps; John knew she was in a happy mood. His steps were heavy and he avoided people, even though it was dark. But why should he feel ashamed? The girl was beautiful, probably the most beautiful girl in the whole of Limuru. Yet he feared being seen with her. It was all wrong. He knew that he could have loved her; even then he wondered if he did not love her. Perhaps it was hard to tell but, had he been one of the young men he had met, he would not have hesitated in his answer.

Outside the village he stopped. She, too, stopped. Neither had spoken a word all through. Perhaps the silence spoke louder than words. Both of them were only too conscious of each other.

'Do they know?' Silence. Wamuhu was probably considering the question. 'Don't keep me waiting. Please answer me,' he implored. He felt weary, very weary, like an old man who had suddenly reached his journey's end.

'No. You told me to give you one more week. A week is over today.'

'Yes. That's why I came!' John whispered hoarsely.

Wamuhu did not speak. John looked at her. Darkness was now between them. He was not really seeing her; before him was the image of his father – haughtily religious and dominating. Again he thought: I, John, a priest's son, respected by all and going to college, will fall, fall to the ground. He did not want to contemplate the fall.

'It was your fault.' He found himself accusing her. In his heart he knew he was lying.

'Why do you keep on telling me that? Don't you want to marry me?'

John sighed. He did not know what to do. He remembered a story his mother used to tell him. Once upon a time there was a young girl ... she had no home to go to and she could not go forward to the beautiful land and see all the good things because the *Irimu* was on the way ...

'When will you tell them?'

'Tonight.'

He felt desperate. Next week he would go to the college. If he could persuade her to wait, he might be able to get away and come back when the storm and consternation had abated. But then the government might withdraw his bursary. He was frightened and there was a sad note of appeal as he turned to her and said, 'Look, Wamuhu, how long have you been pre- ... I mean, like this?'

'I have told you over and over again, I have been pregnant for three months and mother is being suspicious. Only yesterday she said I breathed like a woman with a child.'

'Do you think you could wait for three weeks more?'

She laughed. Ah! the little witch! She knew his trick. Her laughter always aroused many emotions in him.

'All right,' he said. 'Give me just tomorrow. I'll think up something. Tomorrow I'll let you know.'

'I agree. Tomorrow. I cannot wait any more unless you mean to marry me.'

Why not marry her? She is beautiful! Why not marry? Do I love her or don't I?

She left. John felt as if she was deliberately blackmailing him. His knees were weak and lost strength. He could not move but sank on the ground in a heap. Sweat poured profusely down his cheeks, as if he had been running hard under a strong sun. But this was cold sweat. He lay on the grass; he did not want to think. Oh, no! He could not possibly face his father. Or his mother. Or Reverend Carstone who had had such faith in him. John realised that, though he was educated, he was no more secure than anybody else. He was no better than Wamuhu. Then why don't you marry her? He did not know. John had grown up under a Calvinistic father and learnt under a Calvinistic headmaster – a missionary! John tried to pray. But to whom was he praying? To Carstone's God? It sounded false. It was as if he was blaspheming. Could he pray to the God of the tribe? His sense of guilt crushed him.

He woke up. Where was he? Then he understood. Wamuhu had left him. She had given him one day. He stood up; he felt good. Weakly, he began to walk back home. It was lucky that darkness blanketed the whole earth and him in it. From the various huts, he could hear laughter, heated talks or quarrels. Little fires could be seen flickering red through the open doors. Village stars, John thought. He raised up his eyes. The heavenly stars, cold and distant, looked down on him impersonally. Here and there, groups of boys and girls could be heard laughing and shouting. For them life seemed to go on as usual. John consoled himself by thinking that they, too, would come to face their day of trial.

John was shaky. Why! Why could he not defy all expectations, all prospects of a future, and marry the girl? No. No. It was impossible. She was circumcised and he knew that his father and the church would never consent to such a marriage. She had no learning – or rather she had not gone beyond standard four. Marrying her would probably ruin his chances of ever going to a university.

He tried to move briskly. His strength had returned. His imagination and thought took flight. He was trying to explain his action before an accusing world – he had done so many times before, ever since he knew of this. He still wondered what he could have done. The girl had attracted him. She was graceful and her smile had been very bewitching. There was none who could equal her and no girl in the village had any pretence to any higher standard of education. Women's education was very low. Perhaps that was why so many Africans went 'away' and came back married. He too wished he had gone with the others, especially in the last giant student airlift to America. If only Wamuhu had learning ... and she was uncircumcised ... then he might probably rebel.

The light still shone in his mother's hut. John wondered if he should go in for the night prayers. But he thought against it; he might not be strong enough to face his parents. In his hut the light had gone out. He hoped his father had not noticed it.

John woke up early. He was frightened. He was normally not superstitious, but still he did not like the dreams of the night. He dreamt of circumcision; he had just been initiated in the tribal manner. Somebody – he could not tell his face, came and led him because he took pity on him. They went, went into a strange land. Somehow, he found himself alone. The somebody had vanished. A ghost came. He recognised it as the ghost of the home he had left. It pulled him back; then another ghost came. It was the ghost of the land he had come to. It pulled him forward. The two contested. Then came other ghosts from all sides and pulled him from all sides so that his body began to fall into pieces. And the ghosts were insubstantial. He could not cling to any. Only they were pulling him and he was becoming nothing, nothing ... he was now standing a distance away. It had not been him. But he was looking at the girl, the girl in the story. She had nowhere to go. He thought he would go to help her; he would show her the way. But as he went to her, he lost his way ... he was all alone ... something destructive was coming towards him, coming, coming ... He woke up. He was sweating all over.

Dreams about circumcision were no good. They portended death. He dismissed the dream with a laugh. He opened the window only to find the whole country clouded in mist. It was perfect July weather in Limuru. The hills, ridges, valleys and plains that surrounded the village were lost in the mist. It looked such a strange place. But there was almost a magic fascination in it. Limuru was a land of contrasts and evoked differing emotions at different times. Once John would be fascinated and would yearn to touch the land, embrace it or just be on the grass. At another time he would feel repelled by the dust, the strong sun and the pot-holed roads. If only his struggle were just against the dust, the mist, the sun and the rain, he might feel content. Content to live here. At least he thought he would never like to die and be buried anywhere else but at Limuru. But there was the human element whose vices and betrayal of other men were embodied in the new ugly villages. The last night's incident rushed into his mind like a flood, making him weak again. He got out of his blankets and went out. Today he would go to the shops. He was uneasy. An odd feeling was coming to him – in fact had been coming – that his relationship with his father was perhaps unnatural. But he dismissed the thought. Tonight would be the day of reckoning. He shuddered to think of it. It was unfortunate that this scar had come into his life at this time, when he was going to Makerere and it would have brought him closer to his father.

They went to the shops. All day long, John remained quiet as they moved from shop to shop buying things from the lanky but wistful Indian traders. And all day long, John wondered why he feared his father so much. He had grown up fearing him, trembling whenever he spoke or gave commands. John was not alone in this.

Stanley was feared by all.

He preached with great vigour, defying the very Gates of Hell. Even during the Emergency, he had gone on preaching, scolding, judging and condemning. All those who were not saved were destined for hell. Above all, Stanley was known for his great and strict moral observances – a bit too strict, rather pharisaical in nature. None noticed this; certainly not the sheep he shepherded. If an elder broke any of the rules, he was liable to be expelled, or excommunicated. Young men and women, seen standing together 'in a manner prejudicial to church and God's morality' (they were one anyway) were liable to be excommunicated. And so, many young men tried to serve two masters by seeing their girls at night and going to church by day. The alternative was to give up church-going altogether.

Stanley took a fatherly attitude to all the people in the village. You must be strict with what is yours. And because of all this he wanted his house to be a good example of this to all. That is why he wanted his son to grow upright. But motives behind many human actions may be mixed. He could never forget that he had also fallen before his marriage. Stanley was also a product of the disintegration of the tribe due to the new influences.

The shopping did not take long. His father strictly observed the silences between them and neither by word nor by hint did he refer to last night. They reached home and John was thinking that all was well when his father called him.

'John.'

'Yes, Father.'

'Why did you not come for prayers last night?'

'I forgot ...'

'Where were you?'

Why do you ask me? What right have you to know where I was? One day I am going to revolt against you. But, immediately, John knew that this act of rebellion was something beyond him – unless something happened to push him into it. It needed someone with something he lacked.

'I – I – I mean, I was ...'

'You should not sleep so early before prayers. Remember to turn up tonight.'

'I will.'

Something in the boy's voice made the father look up. John went away relieved. All was still well.

Evening came. John dressed like the night before and walked with faltering steps towards the fatal place. The night of reckoning had come. And he had not thought of anything. After this night all would know. Even Reverend Carstone would hear of it. He remembered Reverend Carstone and the last words of blessing he had spoken to him. No! he did not want to remember. It was no good remembering these things; and yet the words came. They were clearly written in the air, or in the darkness of his mind. 'You are going into the world. The world is waiting even like a hungry lion, to swallow you, to devour you. Therefore, beware of the world. Jesus said, Hold fast unto ...' John felt a pain – a pain that wriggled through his flesh as he remembered these words. He contemplated the coming fall. Yes! He, John, would fall from the Gates of Heaven down through the open waiting Gates of Hell. Ah! He could see it all, and all that people would say. All would shun his company, all would give him oblique looks that told so much. The trouble with John was that his imagination magnified the fall from the heights of 'goodness' out of all proportion. And fear of people and consequences ranked high in the things that made him contemplate the fall with so much horror.

John devised all sorts of punishment for himself. And when it came to thinking of a way out, only fantastic and impossible ways of escape came into his head. He simply could not make up his mind. And because he could not, and because he feared Father and people and did not know his true attitude to the girl, he came to the agreed spot having nothing to tell her. Whatever he did looked fatal to him. Then suddenly he said:

'Look, Wamuhu. Let me give you money. You might then say that someone else was responsible. Lots of girls have done this. Then that man may marry you. For me, it is impossible. You know that.'

'No. I cannot do that. How can you, you ...'

'I will give you two hundred shillings.'

'No!'

'Three hundred.'

'No!' She was almost crying. It pained her to see him so.

'Four hundred, five hundred, six hundred.' John had begun calmly but now his voice was running high. He was excited. He was becoming more desperate. Did he know what he was talking about? He spoke

A Meeting in the Dark

quickly, breathlessly, as if he was in a hurry. The figure was rapidly rising – nine thousand, ten thousand, twenty thousand ... He is mad. He is foaming. He is quickly moving towards the girl in the dark. He had lain his hands on her shoulders and is madly imploring her in a hoarse voice. Deep inside him, something horrid that assumes the threatening anger of his father and the village seems to be pushing him. He is violently shaking Wamuhu, while his mind tells him that he is patting her gently. Yes, he is out of his mind. The figure has now reached fifty thousand shillings and is increasing. Wamuhu is afraid. She extricates herself from him, the mad, educated son of a religious clergyman, and runs. He runs after her and holds her, calling her by all sorts of endearing words. But he is shaking her, shake, shake, her, her – he tries to hug her by the neck, presses ... she lets out one horrible scream and then falls on the ground. And so all of a sudden, the struggle is over, the figures stop, and John stands there trembling like the leaf of a tree on a windy day.

Soon everyone will know that he has created and then killed.

Revision questions

1. a) How do members of John's family namely John himself, his father Stanley and his mother Susana relate to one another?
   b) Are they a happy family?
   c) Why do you think they all use Christian names?
2. With reference to Susana and Wamuhu and her mother, show how Ngugi portrays women.
3. a) With varied illustrations from the story, show how the villagers regarded John.
   b) What reactions did John's visit to Wamuhu's parents draw from:
      i) Wamuhu's father
      ii) Wamuhu's mother?
4. a) Explain John's dream about ghosts.
   b) How does it bring out the predicament he is in?
   c) What does it portend for his future?
5. Describe the characters of John, Stanley his father and that of Wamuhu's father.
6. How does Ngugi use suspense to hold our interest in this story?

Topics for discussion

1. 'The trouble with John was that his imagination magnified the fall from the heights of 'goodness' out of all proportion.' How did this lead to what John did to Wamuhu?
2. a) If you were John, would you have acted the way he did?
   b) What is the best way to act when you face a predicament?

3 What is ironical about John's final action?
4 Refer to the story *The Martyr*. What similarities do you find in:
   a) The development of the characters of John and Njoroge
   b) The description of events?

Fatmata Conteth
Ethiopia

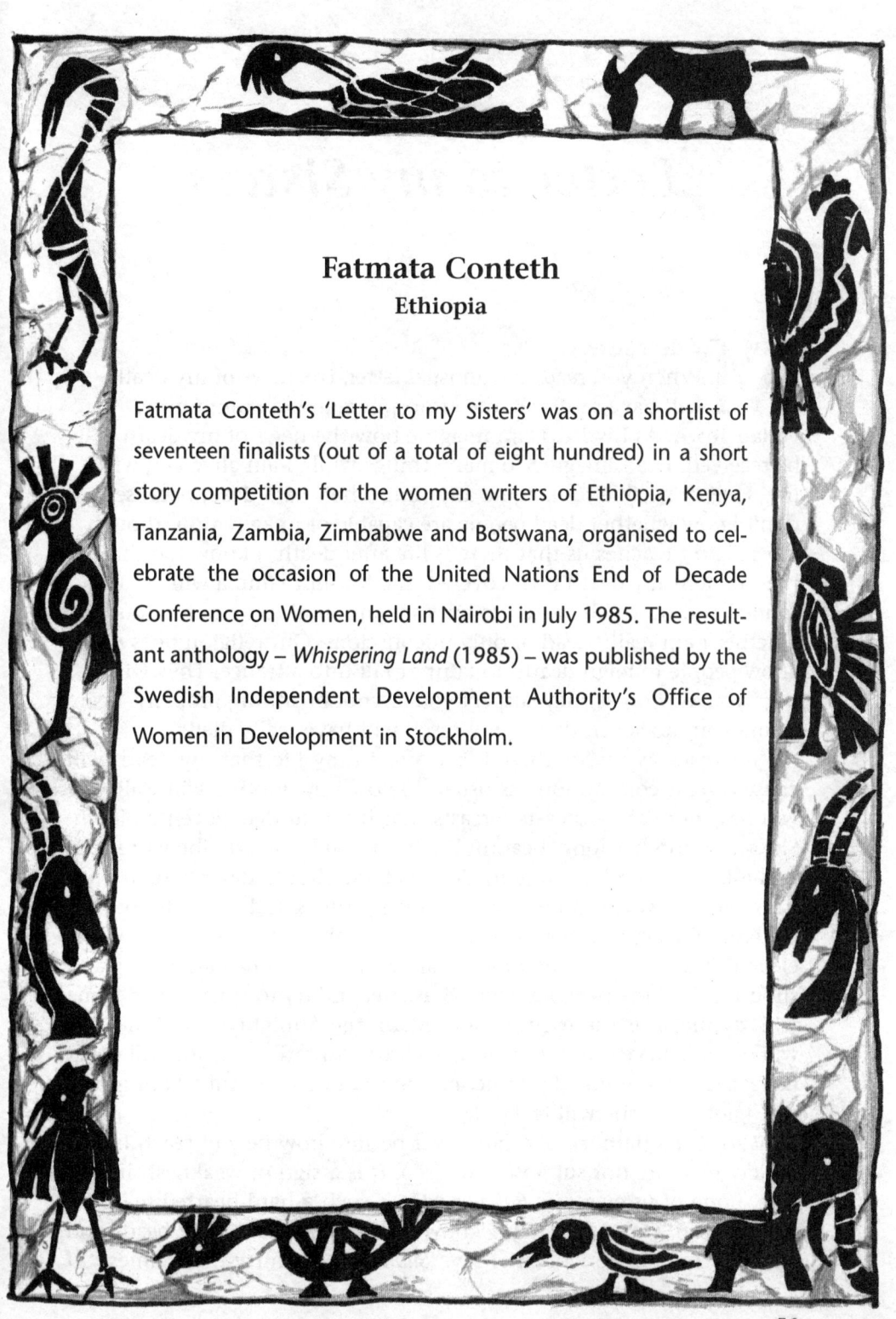

Fatmata Conteth's 'Letter to my Sisters' was on a shortlist of seventeen finalists (out of a total of eight hundred) in a short story competition for the women writers of Ethiopia, Kenya, Tanzania, Zambia, Zimbabwe and Botswana, organised to celebrate the occasion of the United Nations End of Decade Conference on Women, held in Nairobi in July 1985. The resultant anthology – *Whispering Land* (1985) – was published by the Swedish Independent Development Authority's Office of Women in Development in Stockholm.

Letter to my Sisters

My dear sisters,
When you read this unusual letter, the news of my death will have saturated the atmosphere in our community, Fullah Town. As I write, I can imagine how the news of my death will be received. I can imagine so many things while I am alive and writing. I won't be able to imagine anything when I am dead, because I don't know whether dead people are capable of imagination, though our religion teaches us that there is life after death. I know too that the moment my death is discovered, the Muslim Jamma will be summoned and they will hasten to bury me, not bothering to find out whether I am really dead or only unconscious. Our religion does not allow people to feign death, to faint or fall into a trance. They will bury you as soon as they suspect you are not breathing properly. I can assure you, however, that in my case I will have really died.

I do know as I write these last words in my life that my death will cause a great commotion. As usual, I know how mother will wail. She will beat her flabby breasts. Breasts that have suckled eleven children. She will undo her long, beautiful hair and pull it apart. She will shout and ask what she has done to God that she should deserve such punishment. She will call my name countless times and she will ask why God should deprive her of her eldest daughter and the fifth of her eleven children, why only nine are alive. She will run about, crying and shouting, and many women will chase her and try to console her. Some will say that it is the wish of God, Allah, the Almighty, that I die. She will never believe that I took my own life voluntarily. No, she will never believe it because suicide is uncommon in our community. Poor mother, I know how she will feel.

As for *Baba* (father), one can never be sure how he will react. In our society men are not supposed to weep. It is a sign of weakness. In any case, none of us ever saw *Baba* cry. He is such a hard-hearted man. He will feel sad, very sad. Then I know he will grab his prayer beads and start his *Tasbih*. He will then say, '*Subhanallah*' thirty-three times, '*Al

Hamudu Lillah' thirty-three times, '*Allahu-Akbar* (Allah is the Greatest)' thirty-four times. Indeed, *Baba* will say, '*Allahu-Akbar, Allahu-Akbar,* Allah is the Greatest, Allah is the Greatest,' many times. And his peers, some of the neighbours will come and sit by him and say exactly what *Baba* is saying. But *Baba* will not weep. He believes so much in his manhood, his religion and God and the total submission of women to men and their parents. He will say I died because it is the will of Allah, the Greatest. He will tell people to hurry and bury me before it is too late. So the whole community will be busy. People will assemble in and around our house, talking about me and my accomplishments. Many will not accept my death as a finality.

My aunts will be full of grief. They are so proud of me. They will curse the day I was born. They will swear I never killed myself. Some will want to accuse some of my stepmothers, especially Mama Janeba who never really liked me that much. They will make all sorts of innuendos against Mama Janeba, poor her. I wish I had a way to defend her. But that is the price she will have to pay for disliking me.

As for my uncles, they will behave like *Baba*. They will be sad, but will not cry. Everything will be attributed to Allah. They will pray and feel justified that they had opposed our going to acquire Western education. They will tell *Baba* how mistaken he was in allowing us to go to school. Islamic education was enough for us as they had advocated.

I know how you my sisters will react to the news of my death. You will cry like Mama. Your eyes will be red and they will bulge. I know how Intuma will sing while weeping. She will say she has lost her eldest sister. She will clap her hands, put her hands on her head and run around. She will say she would like to accompany me. Her world, she will say, has come to an end. She will ask who killed our sister. She will talk about her sister who was the first female Muslim girl to get a university education and then to have gone to the white man's country to become the first female medical doctor in the Fullah Town community.

As for Amina, she will just gnash her teeth. She will probably go into a trance. It will take her a long time to believe. She will believe days later, after my funeral, otherwise she will think I will come back to life.

After a while, she will say to herself that she must stop crying. That it is God's will. Isha will take over from her. She will say that someone killed her sister. She will say that she knows the person. But she will never call names of suspects. She will cry for a long time. In the end, she will lose her voice and her speech will be incomprehensible for some time. As for Ajaratu, she will leave the compound and run towards the stream. Then people will chase her for fear she might drown herself or do some other harm to herself. After a while they will bring her back, sandwiched in the arms of people. People will crowd around to console her. I know how all of you, my sisters, will react, but I cannot name all seventeen of you in this short letter.

As for our brothers, they are no different from *Baba* and all our uncles. But I think that the little boys will cry. They will all cry because they will remember what I used to do for all of them at the end of Ramadan month and on Christmas. They will miss the presents that I used to work so hard to get for them just to make them happy. The older brothers will probably hate me for killing myself. They will never stop to think, to understand and appreciate why I did what I did. But that is their business, they are all just like *Baba*, full of their manhood.

The dailies will have various captions. I can imagine such headlines as, 'Dr Dao commits suicide', 'Fullah Town has lost its first female doctor.' Some will say, 'Suicide, Dr Dao dead.' Some papers will suspect foul play until the facts are known. But that is what should be expected. It is normal.

In the hospital where I work, my colleagues and my patients will react likewise. Many of my colleagues have always said that I am too reserved for their comfort. Some think it is because I am a Muslim. Some think that it is because I am in a profession which is traditionally male. I never told them the reason for my apparent reserve. My patients would be shocked and baffled. I can imagine how Ya-Yanoh will feel. Remember sisters, I always tell you about Ya-Yanoh, the woman with a big ulcer on her left thigh. In her village they say that her ulcer is incurable because she is said to be a witch. She also believes that and has become very miserable. She is insulted by all and sundry and her situation is made worse by the fact that she is childless. When I admitted her, she narrated her ordeal to me and I told her I would help her to get well. She could not believe it. At the time of writing this letter, she is in the process of getting discharged. Her sore is healed, completely. I remember when I used to go on my rounds in the wards. She was my favourite patient. I treated her like our mother. She told me I had restored her dignity and respect. So when she returns to her village, walking straight and confident, people will regard her as a human being. Before that she was treated with contempt and opprobrium.

Sometimes, after listening to her stories, I felt like crying. She is a nice woman after all. One thing I remember about her is her teeth. They are very clean and almost intact. Because of this also, she said people accused her of witchcraft. According to people in her village, she said, a woman of her age ought to have few teeth. So her life was one full of torment. How she will cry when news of my death reaches her.

Amina and Ajara will recall the lady who said that I am the only female doctor she ever knew and how happy that made her. She used to say that even if she died, she would have had the satisfaction of having known a female doctor. She was joking, of course. I like her all the same.

Fatmata Conteth

She is one of my favourites. She appreciates the fact that we work hard and make lots of sacrifices, especially those who have night duty. But then she would say that had she been a doctor she would not have liked night duty because she wants to be with her husband. Then she would laugh and the other patients would join in her laughter. She is such fun. She too will cry and feel very sad.

My dear sisters, I know that you will want to know why I took my life. Well, it is a long story. Partly, I am doing it for your sakes. I did it so that you can get freedom. For this, I have to sacrifice my life to set you free, you and your daughters and your daughters' daughters.

You may not understand now. However, as you read along, as you get to the end of this letter, I am sure you will understand and appreciate my action. You may not approve of this method of helping you to be free, to be women of dignity, pride and self-esteem. I have taken what I consider a courageous course of action to assert my dignity and yours too. I am writing this unusual letter to justify my action to be free. I hope I am also helping women of my community. If I fail to tell you the reason for my action, some of you will never forgive me. This is why I am writing the story of my life to you, my younger sisters. I owe it to you as a moral duty, to tell you the truth, nothing but the truth.

From the time I was a little child, *Baba* was always concerned about upholding the family name of the Daos. The upholding of the family name transcends everything in *Baba's* life. The respectability and reverence which the name Dao enjoys should never be allowed to diminish. But from the time I can remember things correctly, it had appeared that the upholding of the family name was the sole responsibility of us girls. The fact that our great grandfather was among the few Imams of the mosque of Fullah Town has served to enslave us rather than make us free people. You know how people talk about us. We should not say certain things because we are of the Dao family. The things that normal people do we cannot do. We are a very religious family. But above all we are women; so we hold the family name in trust.

As you know, we went to the Koranic school at an early age and finished in record time, before our brothers – both the elder and the younger ones. We always did better than they did. *Baba*, as you all know, was against our going to school to get Western education. He was more inclined to allow the boys rather than us. His argument was the usual and familiar one, to which our uncles, apart from one, also subscribe. Girls should get married and have children. Western education, he had observed, bred immorality, disrespect for elders and for tradition. That he finally allowed us to go to school was due to the influence of one of our uncles, Uncle Bubu. But that is not surprising. Uncle Bubu is the most educated and enlightened of them all. That he went to school was an accident of history. So he knows what education means. We all thanked him for what he did for us. But that was a long time ago.

In school we did better than all our brothers. Even the eldest never reached my standard. We all know how Nkodo Shaifu, from our own point of view, brought dishonour to this family. He had had children out of wedlock. *Baba* was not offended. He was happy he had grandchildren. Worst of all, Nkodo had had these children while still at school. He could not pass his examinations to go to college. That, to me, is a shame. *Baba* never thought it was dishonourable. It was Uncle Bardara who felt somewhat embarrassed by the incident.

Do you still recall our big secret? No one, as far as I know, can forget that incident. I am referring to the time Ajara almost died while trying to induce abortion. We had all been so terrified that if it became known that one of us had been made pregnant out of wedlock, it would have brought dishonour to the Dao family. Ajara almost lost her life. I hope all of you are beginning to understand what I am trying to point out to you.

Have we not lamented many times that we are not allowed out of the house except when accompanied by several of our younger brothers and sisters? You know that we must always come home much earlier than even our younger brothers. You also know how we are watched. Our friends are even chosen for us. That applied to me too as an elder sister. That was how I found myself the centre of ridicule, because by the time I went to college I did not know how to dance. I found it difficult to socialise. My friends used to say I had two left feet. I learned to dance much later in life when I was in England studying medicine. I was afraid of men, because I was afraid they would ask me out to parties. I must confess that I was miserable.

Have you girls noticed how our younger brothers can dance to all sorts of music? *Baba* would only say with delight that they are men.

You all remember the incident when *Baba* threatened to disown me. I am referring to the day I wore trousers. I had just come from England and thought I had grown out of that type of family control. *Baba* said it was a big shame, a dishonour to the family for a girl, his daughter, to put on trousers. 'This was why I said that Western education breeds immorality. You have come here now to teach your own younger sisters bad manners. God have mercy on you. I tell you, hell fire will consume you for this!' He had even scolded mother. It was mother who had given birth to somebody like me. Hell fire, he said, will also consume mother. According to him, hell was not comparable to anything we knew of on earth. He always threatened us with hell fire. That day, *Baba* was very angry with me. He even threatened to set fire to me if he ever saw me in trousers again. I always damn that day when I think of it. It was a terrible day. Mother wept later for me. Poor mother, she weeps for everything. I felt guilty as though I had committed a crime.

I always thought women could wear trousers in Islamic countries. *Baba* said I was to dress like a woman. He meant perhaps for me to tie a wrappa. To tie a wrappa, and to do work, I thought. Whenever I looked into my wardrobe and glanced at my beautiful trousers, I felt pain in my stomach. The thought that I could never put them on while I was under the regime of *Baba* made me feel sick.

Home has become hell for me. No boyfriend would dare call me or come to our house. When I had intimated to *Baba* that the government had provided me with a house, he told me I would leave his house only on my way to my matrimonial home. I wept bitterly. Mother wept too. For *Baba*, unmarried girls should not live by themselves. It is immoral. But it is all right for our brothers to live by themselves. That would not bring dishonour to the family. My God! So I accepted in disbelief.

'Why then did I have to spend so much of my time going to college?' I asked myself. I would have been like our mother. Mama accepted and believed that she was born to serve *Baba* or any man that would have her as a wife. Mama could never question anything *Baba* said to her, good or bad. Mama, whose once seductive figure had now become lost in fat, because *Baba* had scolded her that she was giving him a bad name by staying slim. *Baba* likes fat women. So Mama became fat. I once told her that from a professional point of view her fat would kill her. I meant it. She laughed and ignored me. 'If you disobey your husband, you will not go to heaven.' She was sure and very serious about it. I laughed and Mama thought I was stupid.

You all remember when we wanted to talk to Uncle Bardara. We wanted to talk to him so that he could talk to his brother to allow us freedom of movement, speech and association. We hesitated. It was difficult to trust Uncle Bardara also. We saw him beat his wives very often for minor offences. One day he beat one of his wives until the woman vomited. Her crime had been that she had gone to watch masquerade devils. For Uncle Bardara, it was the devil that had induced his wife. So he had decided to beat the hell out of her, as our people would say. In many ways, Uncle Bardara is like *Baba*. Many people also like *Baba* because he is said to be very religious. He knows the Koran and quotes from it with ease, which has earned him the envy of his peers. He has visited the Holy City of Mecca several times and this also adds to the reverence people have for him. He looks like someone incapable of hurting a fly. His countenance is deceptive, very deceptive.

We could not appeal to *Baba's* best friend. He is a lamentably dull man who cannot offer *Baba* the intellectual stimulation *Baba* always seeks from his colleagues.

My world then became a prison, a closed world. Sometimes I feel guilty even just talking to men. I feel my father's curse will affect me. I have contemplated rebellion many times. But again, I have been taught that an outright act of rebellion against any of one's parents is sinful. I am afraid.

Do you remember when our elder brother searched my wardrobe after money and inadvertently came across a letter from a boyfriend of mine? You remember how he read my letter and reported the matter to *Baba*? You know that his emphasis was on these sentences: 'I got attracted to you because of your brown eyes, beautifully framed features and exquisitely contoured body which makes men stare at you when you walk. You are also as brilliant as you are beautiful.' He was vexed. He had already assumed the role of *Baba*. Can all of you imagine? Our lives would be regimented from morning to evening. I know as well as you do that Nkodo will be a worse tyrant than Baba. Most tyrants in history are mediocres. They are also either of average height or below. Well, look at *Baba* and Nkodo, they are of the same height, barely five feet five inches tall.

What then is our future? Amina, that question is for you. Of all my sisters, it is you who will say that, despite my feelings, I should not have taken the action I have taken. Maybe you are right. Well, wait until you get to be my age. Wait until you qualify. I hope, however, that by the time you finish reading this letter, your view will support mine. I really hope so. I do not want to feel that the action I am taking will have been in vain. I hope you feel that life is worth living and not something you should endure.

As the Christians rightly pointed out, Jesus died to make us free. You can only be of use to yourself and to mankind if you are free. I mean if you are free to move, to associate, to talk, to feel inner harmony and a sense of worth. That is exactly what we have not been able to achieve.

Exactly five days ago, a meeting was held. *Baba* had summoned many elders and family members. Unknown to me, they agreed that I should marry the son of Alhaji Hamsu. The decision was final. You all know Alhaji Hamsu's son, the head teacher at the Islamic school. You remember how we used to make fun of him. His head, we would say, when shaved, looked like a mango seed. Then all of us would laugh. He is even older than our elder brother. He has two wives. I am supposed to be wife number three, because we are all Muslims. *Baba* said he comes from a noble family. Their great grandfather was also among the few who became Imam of Fullah Town Mosque. These are all the considerations. Mama unfortunately is in favour, because she has no choice.

Yes, I am to marry Alhaji Hamsu's son, the fat man. As fat as a bundle. Fat and clumsy. He has created around him an aura of innocent vulnerability. Perhaps that is why *Baba* likes him as a husband for me. But despite this deception, like our Uncle Bardara, he beats his wives and children with efficient brutality.

I know that Amina and Aisha would laugh at this. You will think it is a big joke. We are so incompatible that I find it difficult to believe that *Baba* did this without consulting me. So I asked myself whether I was born never to make a choice, never to enjoy freedom, never to be happy.

Now I am to move to another house of exile, to serve a worse master, to be enslaved again. To say no would be to bring dishonour to the family. To accept is to compromise my freedom. So what is my choice? If I had told mother that I would not accept such a proposal, she would have ordered me to repeat 'Asterfulai', seven times, because I am not supposed to refuse whatever my father proposes or wishes, even as an adult. I do not know what is good for me. Women do not know what is good for them. Imagine any of you, my sisters, being a wife of Alhaji Hamsu's eldest son. Our mother married *Baba* because, in their time, their own concept of marriage was different from ours. Things have changed, you know. We should not be standing still while others are moving. Everybody has a right to be happy, to be free, to love someone of his or her choice, irrespective of family name or religion. It is because of these considerations that I have decided not to enter into such a relationship, organised by *Baba* and others. I have decided not to move from one prison house into another for the rest of my life. If this act of defiance robs me of the Kingdom of Heaven, I am prepared to explain myself to Allah the Greatest. I am sure there is justice and freedom in Heaven.

The time I have set for myself is near, the time for my departure. I know that death is painful. Many have died before me in this world because they believed in a cause. Many more will die for ideas and principles they believe in. Many have died, indeed, because they want society to unchain its victims. It is honourable to die because of such convictions. It is by the death of such people that society will be free.

As you know, sisters, for me the world has been a rugged terrain for most of my life. I hope that as a result of my action you will in time enjoy the softer terrain of this world. Do not despair, but do not be complacent either.

The moment is coming nearer. The minutes are moving faster. I am now coming to the end of my letter. The room is hot. There is a breeze but not enough to make the place cool. As usual, I can smell some of the concoctions in Baba's room. He is probably awake, making all sorts of things for his numerous clients. Or maybe he is awake, praying. He could also be just reading his Koran. The smell from his room is very fresh.

Mother is fast asleep. I am sure she hopes to see me in the morning.

She will come to wake me up. She will come to say, 'N'damba my daughter, are you not going to work today?' Then I will reply, 'No, Mama, today is my day off.' Then she will go and prepare breakfast. Breakfast that is always like a feast in this house.

I am now looking at my wardrobe. It is full of all sorts of clothes. Clothes that all of you have always admired and wished to have and wear. But where do you wear them to? To the office? I look at my many trousers and shoes. They are so nice. But of what use are they if they cannot be worn in freedom? I cannot wear them in *Baba's* house. It would have been worse at Alhaji Hamsu's son's house. Now, as I look at them, I feel happy, I enjoy them, I enjoy the feeling of possession. It is a wonderful feeling.

Finally, my dear sisters, it is said in the Koran that there is life after death. I am not sure about that. Let us hope it is true. If it is true, then we shall meet again. It will be a wonderful reunion. I will be eager to hear the stories of your lives, to know if they were different from mine. Then we shall make merry eternally and live for ever after.

So, Goodbye.

N'damba.

Revision questions

1. a) What do you learn about the writer's family from her letter?
   b) How do the different sexes and ages in the family relate to one another?
   c) Who seems most disadvantaged and why?
2. Giving reasons, show how the death of the writer will affect:
   a) the womenfolk
   b) the men
   c) her patients and colleagues?
3. a) What reasons does Dr Dao, the writer, give for her decision to take her own life?
   b) Do you think she made the right decision?
   c) What else should she have done instead of making such a decision?
4. Do other women in the story hold the same opinion as the writer in respect to the predicament all women face?
5. a) Why is the writer a very important person in her community?
   b) Does the community appreciate that importance? Why or why not?
6. What do you learn about the community's attitude towards:
   i) marriage
   ii) education?
   Do you agree with them?

7 Describe three incidents to show what happened to the writer when she behaved contrary to the expectations of her family.
8 Why doesn't the writer want to marry the husband her father has chosen for her?
9 a) Discuss the character of the writer.
  b) Identify two other characters who you think are developed and describe them.

Topics for discussion

1 a) Why do you think the writer decides to convey her message by writing a letter rather than talk to her sisters?
  b) Would the message have been as candid and resolute if the story of the writer were told through description?
2 In a class debate, discuss the theme of discrimination against women.
3 a) Discuss the portrayal of gender in Dr Dao's letter.
  b) Are gender roles in your own community any different?
  c) In your opinion how should people of different sexes be treated?

Nawal El Saadawi
Egypt

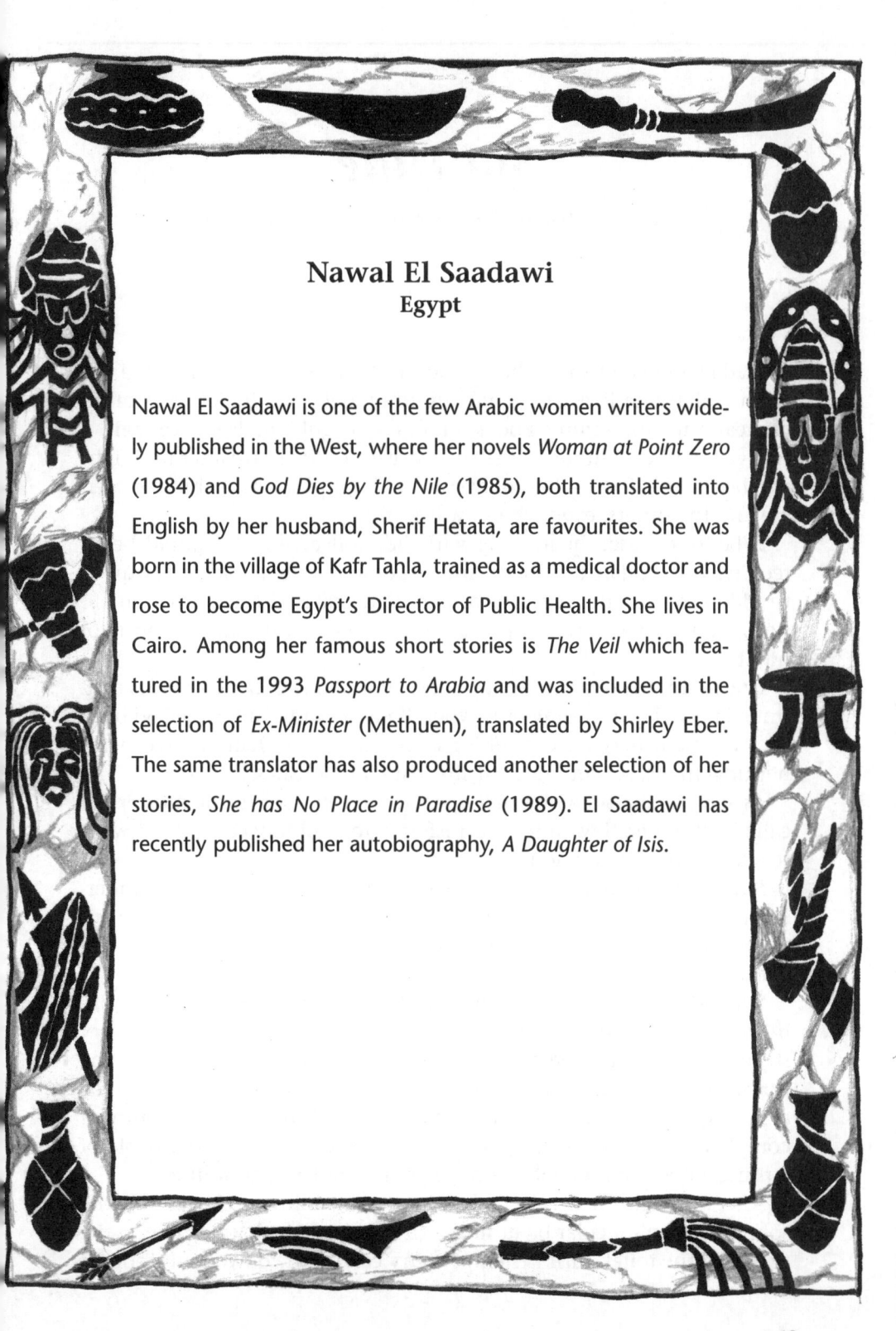

Nawal El Saadawi is one of the few Arabic women writers widely published in the West, where her novels *Woman at Point Zero* (1984) and *God Dies by the Nile* (1985), both translated into English by her husband, Sherif Hetata, are favourites. She was born in the village of Kafr Tahla, trained as a medical doctor and rose to become Egypt's Director of Public Health. She lives in Cairo. Among her famous short stories is *The Veil* which featured in the 1993 *Passport to Arabia* and was included in the selection of *Ex-Minister* (Methuen), translated by Shirley Eber. The same translator has also produced another selection of her stories, *She has No Place in Paradise* (1989). El Saadawi has recently published her autobiography, *A Daughter of Isis*.

Solitude

(Translated from the Arabic by Marilyn Booth)

I had imagined prison to be solitude and total silence, the isolated cell in which one lives alone, talking to oneself, rapping at the wall to hear the responding knock of one's neighbour. Here, though, I enjoyed neither solitude nor silence, except in the space after midnight and before the dawn call to prayer. I could not pull a door shut between me and the others, even when I was in the toilet.

If Boduur ceased quarrelling with her colleagues, she would begin reciting the Qur'an out loud. And if Boduur went to sleep, Fawqiyya would wake up and begin to discuss and orate. If Fawqiyya went to sleep, Boduur would wake up to announce prayer time and the onset of night.

One night, the quarrel between Boduur and one of her comrades continued until dawn, ending only when Boduur fainted after she had been hit by violent nervous convulsions. She tore at her hair and face with her fingernails, screaming until she lost consciousness.

As soon as the shawisha had opened the cell door in the morning, I called out to her, 'I want to be transferred to a solitary cell. I don't want to stay in this cell any longer.'

But the prison administration rejected my request. I came to understand that in prison, torture occurs not through solitude and silence but in a far more forceful way through uproar and noise. The solitary cell continued to float before me like a dream unlikely to be realised.

Since childhood, I've had a passion for solitude. I've not had a room in which I could shut myself off, for the number of individuals in every stage of my life has been greater than the number of rooms in the house. But I have always wrested for myself a place in which I could be alone to write. My ability to write has been linked to the possibility of complete seclusion, of being alone with myself, for I am incapable of writing when I am unable to give myself completely to solitude.

After midnight, when the atmosphere grows calm and I hear only the sound of sleep's regular breathing, I rise from my bed and tiptoe to the corner of the toilet, turn the empty jerry can upside down and sit on its

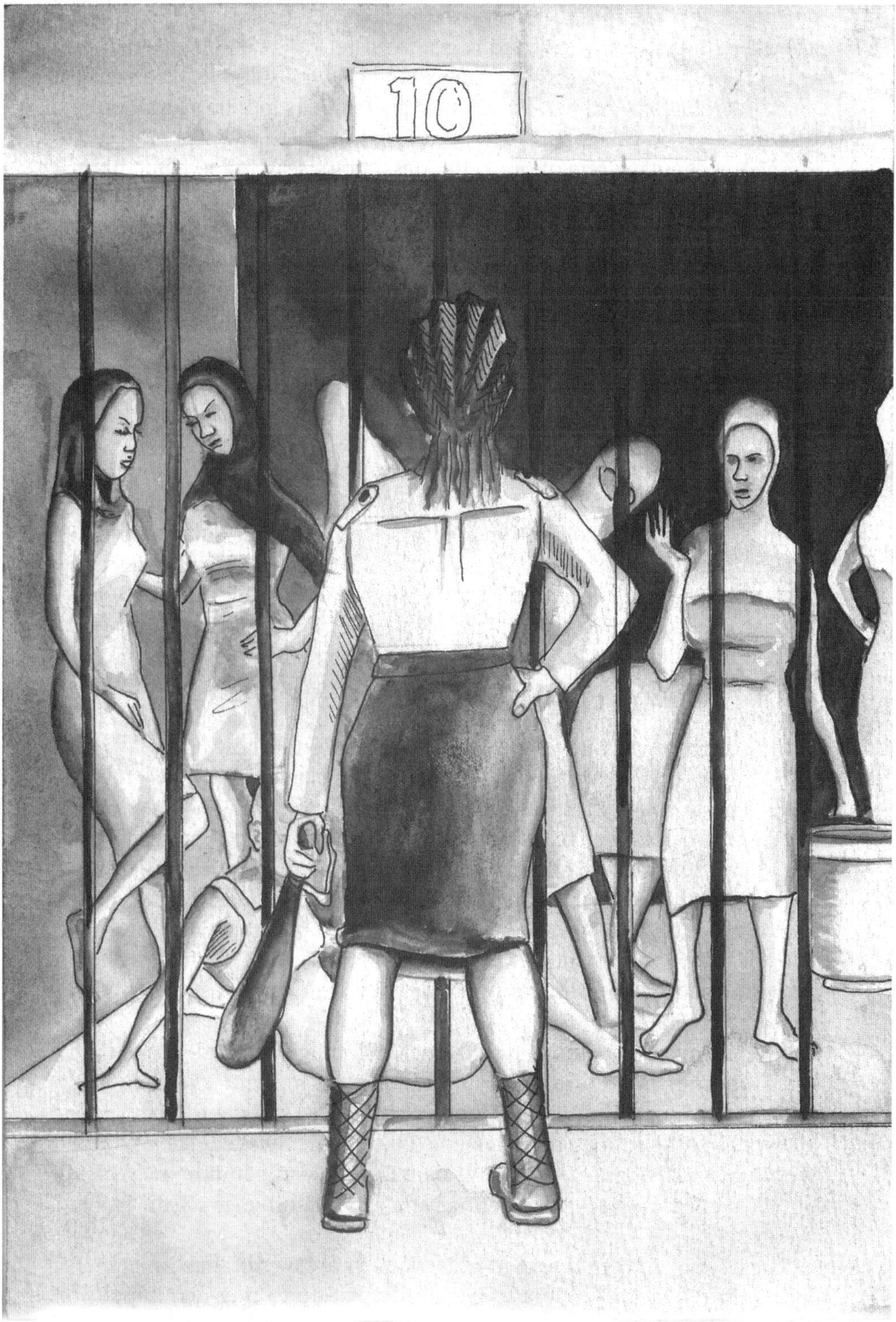
10

bottom. I rest the aluminium plate on my knees, place against it the long, tape-like toilet paper, and begin to write.

In prison, a person's essence comes to light. One stands naked before oneself, and before others. Masks drop and slogans fall. In prison, one's true mettle is revealed, particularly in times of crisis.

The warden gave one of our cellmates a body search and came upon a small piece of paper. It was nothing more than a short letter that she had written to her family, asking after their health and reassuring them of hers. However, the prison administration raged. There must be a pen and paper in the political cell! The search team attacked us – opening suitcases, overturning mattresses, stripping off *higaabs*, *niqaabs*, and cloaks.

One of the *munaqqabas* let out a scream – 'Infidels!' – when they uncovered her hair in front of the male prison administrators. They took her away to the disciplinary cell. From afar, we heard her screaming and we knew they had beaten her. We threatened collectively to go on a hunger strike until she was returned to us, and as a sort of protest against her beating. Collectively, that is, except Boduur and Fawqiyya.

'Going on strike is a type of protest and I do not participate in any protest against the authorities,' said Boduur. 'I do not address the tyrant – I only speak to God. I complain to no one. Complaining to anyone but God is a debasement!'

'They will face the strike by oppressing us still more,' was Fawqiyya's comment.

'Maybe they will put us all in correction cells and beat us.'

However, the group rejected Boduur's logic and that of Fawqiyya alike. The prison regulations do not permit beating or body searches. We must proclaim our rejection of this treatment and our protest. If we are silent this time, our silence will encourage them to repeat the insulting treatment and the beating. Let us use any weapon which we have between our hands. Even if it is merely depriving ourselves of food.

We failed to persuade Boduur. 'There is no point in making any protest,' she said in a tone of finality. 'They are tyrants. God will crush them if it is His wish.'

But Fawqiyya was more frank. The cellmates surrounded her with questions and asked how she could not submit to majority rule, when it was she who had touted the slogan of collective work and sacrifice for the sake of others. She said in a feeble voice, which was unlike any tone we had heard from her previously, 'I am ill and I can't endure the strike.' She lay down on her bed moaning and complaining of a pain in her chest.

The door of the cell opened suddenly and we saw the shawisha entering, followed by our cellmate. We all jumped up to hug her, happy to see her return to us.

Fawqiyya jumped out of bed and embraced her, too, and in the act of leaping she forgot that she was ill.

Before dawn, I awoke to Boduur's voice.

'Get up! Arise for prayer! Prayer is better than sleep!'

'I'm not asleep,' she said in a listless voice. 'I'm sick. They beat me here ... on my head ... Men and women carrying thick, heavy sticks ... I didn't see their faces ... I heard their voices, though ... They pulled off my *niqaab* and *higaab* ... my hair came down in front of them ... I hid it with my hands, my arms. Let them beat me to death but I will not allow men to see my hair! They pulled me by the hair down on to the ground, and put their hands all around my neck so I nearly choked. They stamped on my glasses ... and I can't see at all without my glasses ... I have an awful headache ... my whole body is aching ... my head ... my neck ... my spine ...'

Boduur's voice came back. 'Get up and wash so you can perform the prayer, and don't say that you're ill! Prayer cures you of sickness. It is God who heals. Don't write any complaint to anyone. God is present. If you are innocent, God will make you victorious. Do not say that you didn't do anything wrong: you must have done something sinful in your life and then forgotten about it. God could not possibly expose you to pain or torture or prison or beating without a sin on your part. A human being is always sinful and you must ask God's forgiveness. Repentance is an obligation, whether you've committed a sin or not. Since God has requested us to ask His forgiveness, we must have committed sins. Human beings are sinful by nature – otherwise, there would be no such thing as repentance or forgiveness. Say "I beg God's forgiveness" three times, and get up to pray! You absolutely must stay up all night to pray – the five obligatory prayers are not enough. If you find the water cut off, intention is enough. The religion makes things easy, not difficult, and washing with water is not obligatory. Water is not important. It is important, though, that you keep God in your mind and speech, day and night. Staying up at night to pray is better and more enduring than sleep. You went to the correction cell because you were not staying up at night to pray and because you haven't memorised the Qur'an. I've told you more than once that you must learn two chapters of the Qur'an by heart every week. This is a sacred duty. Whoever does not fulfil it must have her feet whipped fifty times. Who knows, maybe it was God's will that you were beaten by the hands of others so you would atone for your sins. It's not enough that you cover your face with a *niqaab*. You must cleanse your heart of Satan's whisperings. Woman is nearer to Satan than man – through Eve, Satan was able to reach Adam. Woman was created from a crooked rib and she becomes straightened only through blows which hurt. Her duty is to listen and obey without making any objections – even a blink or a scowl. A scowl calls for thirty lashes on the feet.'

I saw the girl rise from her bed. I saw her walk, her back stooped, in the direction of the toilet, groping for a way with her hands, for she had lost her glasses. She put on her cloak and *niqaab* ... and stood behind Boduur, praying and asking God's forgiveness for her sins.

Shawisha Nabawiyya astonished me sometimes by taking courageous stands in which she stood firmly on the side of right and showed no fear of the prison administration's power. Unlike the other shawishas, she did not accept any bribery. Nor did she allow a prisoner to be beaten, even if the senior official in charge ordered her to do so.

'Once I obeyed the order and beat a prisoner in the correction cell,' she said. 'Then I went home, and I felt pain around my heart. I stayed home for a week, sick, and since then I have not beaten any prisoner. Even if they threatened to dismiss me, I would never beat a prisoner. I quarrel with my son when he beats a cat or dog – so what about a human being?'

Boduur was sitting beside her, listening to her words. 'You have a good heart, Shawisha Nabawiyya, and God will reward you well. God has requested us to show gentleness towards animals and human beings and all of God's creatures.'

'Except for one,' I remarked. 'Woman.'

'Why woman?' asked the shawisha.

'Because she was created from a crooked rib,' I replied, 'and only straightens up through beating.' I laughed, and so did the shawisha and the others in the cell – all except Boduur. Without delay, the scowl appeared on her forehead in the form of a deep, vertical line. 'Woman lacks intelligence and religion,' she said.

'And you? Aren't you a woman?' asked the shawisha.

'No!' she shouted.

Revision questions
1. In prison life solitude or solitary confinement is one of the ways prisoners regarded as hardened criminals are punished.
    a) Why did the narrator request to be confined in solitude?
    b) Would you have wished for solitude were you in her shoes?
2. a) What sort of people were Boduur and Fawqiyya?
    b) Did they care for the welfare of fellow prisoners as they claimed?
3. a) What was the profession of the narrator? Give reasons for your answer.
    b) What sort of prisoners were in the narrator's cell? How do you know?

4 a) Why did the prisoners go on strike?
  b) What reason did the narrator give for supporting the strike?
5 'Woman is nearer to Satan than man'.
  a) Where do you think Boduur got this information from?
  b) What information does she give to support her claim?
  c) Do you agree with her?
6 a) Why do you think the narrator laughed as she repeated Boduur's words '... Because she was created from a crooked rib ... and only straightens up through beating'?
  b) Would you support this treatment of women?
7 a) Discuss the characters of:
    i) The narrator
    ii) Boduur
    iii) Shawisha Nabawiyya.
  b) Compare and contrast the characters of the narrator and Shawisha Nabawiyya.

Topics for discussion

1 Compare the treatment of the theme of 'discrimination against women' in this story and in *Letter to my sisters*.
2 'And you? Aren't you a woman?' asked the shawisha.
  'No!' she shouted.
  a) In what way has Boduur shown that she does not have the interest of her fellow women at heart?
  b) Do you think Boduur has understood her religious teaching on the role of women?
3 *Solitude* is a story about women in prison but they seem to be in a 'a prison within a prison'. Discuss.
4 Discuss the use of sarcasm in this story.

Saida Hagi-Dirie Herzi
Somalia

Born in Mogadishu, Somalia, in the 1950s, Saida has a BA in English Literature from King Abdulaziz University in Jeddah, Saudi Arabia (where she currently teaches English) and a Master's degree from the American University in Cairo, Egypt. She is married with two sons and two daughters. *Against the Pleasure Principle*, her first published story, appeared in *Index on Censorship* in 1990.

Against the Pleasure Principle

Rahma was all excitement. Her husband had been awarded a scholarship to one of the Ivy League universities in the United States, and she was going with him. This meant that she was going to have her baby – the first – in the US. She would have the best medical care in the world.

But there was the problem of her mother. Her mother did not want her to go to the US. Rahma was not sure just what it was that her mother objected to but partly, no doubt, she was afraid she would lose Rahma if she let her go. She had seen it happen with other girls who went abroad: most of them did not come back at all and those who did came only to visit, not to stay. And they let it be known that they had thrown overboard the ways of their people and adopted the ways of the outside world – they painted their lips and their faces; they wore western dress; they went about the city laughing and singing outlandish songs; they spoke in foreign languages or threw in foreign words when they spoke the local language; and they generally acted as though they were superior to all those who stayed behind.

Her mother also seemed worried about Rahma having her baby in the US. Rahma had tried and tried again to reassure her that there was nothing to worry about: she would have the best medical attention. Problems, if any, would be more likely to arise at home than there. But it had made no difference. Her mother kept bombarding her with horror stories she had heard from Somali women coming back from the US – the dreadful things that happened to them when they went to US hospitals, above all when they had their babies there.

Like all women in her native setting, Rahma was circumcised, and, according to her mother, that would mean trouble for her when she was going to have a baby unless there was a midwife from her country to help her. Her mother was convinced that US doctors, who had no experience with circumcised women, would not know what to do.

Rahma had never given much thought to the fact that she had been only four years old when it happened, and nineteen years had passed since then. But she did remember.

It had not been her own feast of circumcision but that of her sister, who was nine then. She remembered the feeling of excitement that enveloped the whole house that morning. Lots of women were there, relatives were bringing gifts – sweets, cakes, various kinds of delicious drinks, trinkets. And her sister was the centre of attention. Rahma remembered feeling jealous, left out, whatever it was they were going to do to her sister, she wanted to have it done too. She cried to have it done, cried and cried till the women around her mother relented and agreed to do it to her too. There was no room for fear in her mind: all she could think of was that she wanted to have done to her what they were going to do to her sister so that she too would get gifts, she too would be fussed over.

She remembered the preliminaries, being in the midst of a cluster of women, all relatives of hers. They laid her on her back on a small table. Two of the women, one to the left of her and the other to the right, gently but firmly held her down with one hand and with the other took hold of her legs and spread them wide. A third standing behind her held down her shoulders. Another washed her genitals with a mixture of *melmel* and *hildeed*, a traditional medicine. It felt pleasantly cool. Off to one side several women were playing tin drums. Rahma did not know that the intent of the drums was to drown the screams that would be coming from her throat in a moment.

The last thing she remembered was one of the women, a little knife in one hand, bending over her. The next instant there was an explosion of pain in her crotch, hot searing pain that made her scream like the rabbit when the steel trap snapped its legs. But the din of the drums, rising to a deafening crescendo, drowned her screams, and the women who held her expertly subdued her young strength coiling into a spring to get away. Then she must have passed out, for she remembered nothing further of the operation in which all the outer parts of her small genitals were cut off, lips, clitoris and all, and the mutilated opening stitched up with a thorn, leaving a passage the size of a grain of sorghum.

When she regained consciousness, she was lying on her mat in her sleeping corner, hot pain between her legs. The slightest movement so aggravated the pain that tears would well up in her eyes. She remembered trying to lie perfectly still so as not to make the pain worse.

For some time after the operation she walked like a cripple: her thighs had been tied together so that she could move her legs only from the knees down, which meant taking only the tiniest of steps. People could tell what had happened to her by the way she walked.

And she remembered how she dreaded passing water. She had to do it sitting because she could not squat, and she had to do it with her thighs closed tightly because of the bindings. To ease the pain of urine pushing through the raw wound of the narrow opening, warm water was poured over it while she urinated. Even so, it brought tears to her eyes. In time the pain abated, but urinating had been associated with discomfort for her ever since.

She remembered being told that she had needed only three thorn stitches. Had she been older, it would have taken four, perhaps five, stitches to sew her up properly. There are accepted standards for the size of a girl's opening: an opening the size of a grain of rice is considered ideal; one as big as a grain of sorghum is acceptable. However, should it turn out as big as a grain of maize, the poor girl would have to go through the ordeal a second time. That's what had happened to her sister; she herself had been luckier. When the women who inspected her opening broke out into the high-pitched *mash-harad* with which women in her society signalled joy, or approval, Rahma knew that it had turned out all right the first time.

Rahma's culture justified circumcision as a measure of hygiene, but the real purpose of it, Rahma was sure, was to safeguard the woman's virginity. Why else the insistence on an opening no larger than a grain of sorghum, one barely big enough to permit the passing of urine and of the menstrual blood? An opening as small as that was, if anything, anti-hygienic. No, if the kind of circumcision that was practised in her area had any purpose, it was to ensure that the hymen remained intact. Her society made so much of virginity that no girl who lost it could hope to achieve a decent marriage. There was no greater blow to a man's ego than to find out that the girl he married was not a virgin.

Rahma knew that, except for the first time, it was customary for women to deliver by themselves, standing up and holding on to a hanging rope. But the first time they needed assistance – someone to cut a passage large enough for the baby's passage. That was what so worried Rahma's mother. She did not think a US doctor could be trusted to make the right cut. Not having had any experience with circumcised women he would not know that the only way to cut was upward from the small opening left after circumcision. He might, especially if the baby's head was unusually big, cut upward and downward. How was he to know that a cut towards the rectum could, and probably would, mean trouble for all future deliveries? Nor would he know that it was best for the woman to be stitched up again right after the baby was born. It was, Rahma's mother insisted, dangerous for a circumcision passage to be left open.

When it became obvious that her words of warning did not have the desired effect on Rahma, her mother decided to play her last trump card – the *Kur*, a ritual feast put on, usually in the ninth month of a pregnancy, to ask God's blessing for the mother and the baby about to be born. Friends and relatives came to the feast to offer their good-luck wishes. It was her mother's intention to invite to the *Kur* two women who had had bad experiences with doctors in the US. They would talk about their experiences in the hope that Rahma would be swayed by them and not go away.

The *Kur* feast was held at her mother's place. When the ritual part of it was over and the well-wishers had offered their congratulations, some of the older women, who had obviously been put up to it by her mother, descended on Rahma trying to accomplish what her mother had failed to do – persuade her to put off going away at least until after the baby's birth.

It did not work. From the expression on Rahma's face that was only too obvious. So her mother signalled for the two special guests to do their part. The first, whose name was Hawa, had spent two years in the US as a student. She talked about the problems of a circumcised woman in a society that did not circumcise its women. 'When people found out where I was from,' she told her audience in a whisper, 'they pestered me with questions about female circumcision. To avoid their questions, I told them that I had not been circumcised myself and therefore could not tell them anything about it. But that did not stop them from bugging me with more questions.' The topic of circumcision, she told them, continued to be a source of embarrassment for as long as she was there.

Hawa then talked about her experience at the gynaecologist's office. She had put off seeing a gynaecologist as long as possible, but when she could not put it off any longer, she looked for, and found, a woman doctor, thinking that she would feel more comfortable with a woman. When the doctor started to examine her, Hawa had heard a gasp. The gasp was followed by a few stammering sounds that turned into a question. The doctor wanted to know whether she had got burned or scalded. When Hawa signalled by a shake of her head that she had done neither, the doctor asked her whether she had had an operation for cancer or something, in which the outer parts of her genital had been amputated. Again Hawa denied anything, and to avoid further questions quickly added that the disfigurement which the doctor found so puzzling was the result of circumcision.

At that, Hawa's doctor went on with the examination without further questions. When she was finished, she turned to Hawa once more. 'You had me confused there,' she muttered, more to herself than to Hawa. 'Don't hold my ignorance against me. I have heard and read about circumcision, but you are the first circumcised woman I have seen in my career. I neither knew that it was still practised nor did I have any idea it went so far.

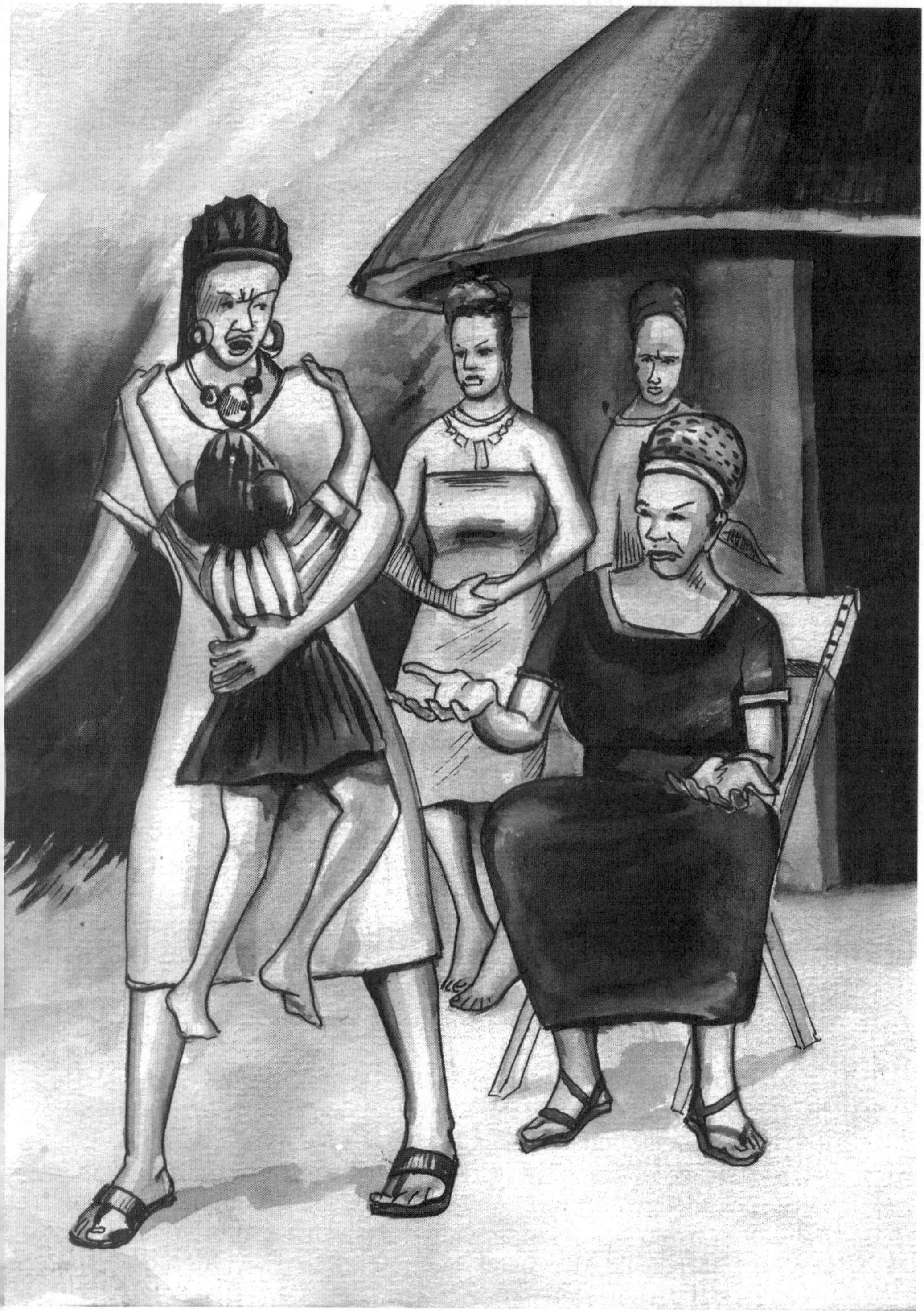

'You know,' she continued after a moment's pause, 'I cannot for the world of me understand why your people have to do this to their women. What misery it must be for a woman sewn up like that to have a baby.'

Hawa said she walked home feeling like a freak: what was left of her genitals must look pretty grim if the sight of it could make a doctor gasp. Why did her people do this to their women? Hundred of millions of women the world over went through life the way God had created them, whole and unmutilated. Why could her people not leave well enough alone? It seemed to her, at least in this case, that man's attempts to improve on nature were a disaster.

The second woman, Dahabo, seemed to believe in circumcision as such. However, when a circumcised woman moved to a part of the world that did not practise circumcision problems were bound to arise. She too had lived in the US. She too had had her encounters with US doctors. She talked at length about her first such encounter. Like Hawa's doctor, hers was a woman; unlike Hawa's hers was familiar with the idea of female circumcision. Nevertheless, Dahabo was her first case of a circumcised woman. Dahabo told her audience about the questioning she was subjected to by her doctor after the examination:

Doctor: Did you have any sort of anaesthesia when they circumcised you?
Dahabo: No, I did not, but I did not really feel any pain because I fainted and remained unconscious during the whole operation.
Doctor: Is circumcision still practised in your culture?
Dahabo: Yes, it is. I had it done to my five-year-old daughter before coming here.
Doctor: Any difference between your way and your daughter's way?
Dahabo: None whatsoever: the same women who circumcised me circumcised her.

At that point, Dahabo told her listeners, something happened that puzzled her: her doctor, eyes full of tears, broke into loud sobs, and she continued to sob while she opened the door to usher her patient out into the corridor. Dahabo said she had never understood what had made her doctor cry.

Rahma had no trouble understanding what it was that had moved the doctor to tears. She was close to tears herself as she left her mother's house to walk home. How much longer, she wondered, would the women of her culture have to endure this senseless mutilation? She knew that, though her people made believe circumcision was a religious obligation, it was really just an ugly custom that had been borrowed from the ancient Egyptians and had nothing to do with Islam. Islam recommends circumcision only for men.

The *Kur* did not achieve what her mother had hoped. Rahma was more determined than ever to accompany her husband to the US. True, there was still the problem of her mother; no doubt her mother meant well, no doubt she wanted the best for her, but Rahma had different ideas about that. She was, for instance, convinced that having her baby in the US was in the best interest of her and of the baby. She would like to have her mother's blessing for the move, but if that was not possible she would go without it. She had always hated circumcision. Now she hated it more than ever. No daughter of hers would ever be subjected to it.

Revision questions
1. How did Rahma get circumcised?
2. What are the dangers of female circumcision to a woman's health?
3. 'It seemed to her, at least in this case, that man's attempts to improve on nature were a disaster'. In what way was circumcision a disaster to Hawa and Dahabo?
4. The two women, Hawa and Dahabo, who had been brought to discourage Rahma from leaving her country did just the opposite. They revealed how negatively outsiders viewed female circumcision. Explain.
5. What is Rahma's own opinion on female circumcision?
6. a) Discuss the characters of: Rahma, her mother, Hawa and Dahabo.
   b) Who of them do you admire most and why?
7. What is the main theme in this story? Discuss it.

Topics for discussion
1. Are you aware of female circumcision? Is it practised in your community? If so, how does it happen?
2. a) Female circumcision is a long standing cultural practice among some communities. Do you support it?
   b) Do you think it is healthy for women?
3. Female circumcision is increasingly being referred to as 'Female Genital Mutilation (F.G.M.).' Using evidence from this story show whether F.G.M. is an appropriate term.
4. Rahma's determination to leave her country symbolises her running away from the cultural practices of her people. Discuss.
5. Think of cultural practices that seem harmful to people. What do you think should be done about such practices?

Government by Magic Spell

At the village

When she was ten, Halima learned that she was possessed by a jinni. The diagnosis came from the religious healer of the village, the *Wadaad*. Halima had been ill for several months. The *Wadaad* had tried all his healing arts on her till he had understood that there could be no cure: Halima was not ill in the ordinary sense of the word; she was possessed – possessed by the spirit of an infant, which she had stepped on by accident, one night in front of the bathroom. Fortunately for Halima, the sage expounded, the jinni was of the benevolent sort, one that was more likely to help than to harm her. But it would never leave her – not leave her voluntarily, not even yield to exorcism. And it would forever be an infant jinni.

With that Halima became famous. The story of her jinni was known from one end of the village to the other within hours after the *Wadaad* had told her mother. Everyone talked about Halima and her jinni – what it might do and what it might be made to do, for her and for the village. In no time at all, the villagers had convinced themselves and each other that Halima had the power to foretell the future and to heal the sick. And it was not long before Halima herself was convinced.

Before long, Halima began to act the part. At times she would sit staring off into space. People assumed that she was listening to her jinni. Or she would actually go into a trance – she would talk, though no one was there to talk to; she would shout at the top of her voice and sometimes she would even cry. Those who witnessed these scenes were filled with holy dread. All were careful not to disturb Halima, during those moments or at any other time, for fear that they might offend the jinni. If people talked about Halima they did so in whispers, behind her back.

Halima made believe that the spirits of the infant's parents visited her during those moments of trance. They came to enquire of the infant, she told people, came to teach her how she could make the jinni happy. At the same time, Halima affirmed, they told her all manner of things about life in general, about the people of the village, things past, things present and things yet to come.

A question that was on the minds of many people in the village was who was to marry Halima when she reached the marriageable age. No one doubted that she would marry. It was what women were for – marriage and childbearing. But there was the problem of the jinni. Wouldn't it be dangerous to be married to a woman possessed? Would there be men brave enough to want to marry Halima?

When Halima did reach the marriageable age, a problem presented itself which no one had anticipated. Halima did not want to get married. There were indeed men brave enough to want to marry her, but Halima turned them all down. The *Wadaad* himself proposed to her. He, people thought, would have been the ideal husband for Halima: he, if anyone, should have been able to cope with a woman possessed. But Halima turned him down too.

Not that possession by a jinni spirit was something unusual in Halima's village. Stories of jinnis abounded – of people who were actually possessed by jinnis, of people who had jinni spirits that were like invisible twin brothers, or people who had jinni spirits as servants. It was common knowledge that one of Halima's own forefathers had had a jinni twin brother called Gess Ade, and one of her mother's grandfathers had had, in addition to a jinni twinbrother, three devoted jinni servants called Toore, Gaadale, and Toor-Ourmone respectively. When Halima's mother had problems, she called on those three for help and protection. The ancestors of several clans were believed to have been born twins, a jinni being the twin partner of each of them. The tribe of Halima's brother-in-law had a twin jinni by the name of Sarhaan.

When animals were sacrificed, the jinni twins had to get their share. In return, the jinnis were expected to give support and protection to the clan. First the animals would be butchered. Then, the ritual songs having been sung, the carcases would be cut open and the inner organs removed. These were to be given to the jinnis. Admonitions would be mumbled such as 'Let's not forget Gess Ade's share; or Toore's, Gaadale's, Ourmone's ...'

The parts set aside for the jinnis would be taken to a remote place up in the hills, and, because they invariably and mysteriously disappeared, the villagers were sure that the jinnis devoured them. No one, therefore, would dream of cheating the jinnis of their share. This had been so for generations and would continue to be so. Children were made to memorise the ritual songs so as to keep the ancestral rites intact from generation to generation.

When Halima was under the spell of her spirits, all her emotions seemed intensified. She experienced a feeling of power, as though she could do things beyond the reach of ordinary human beings. She felt good then. Moreover, whatever she undertook, her spirits seemed to lend a helping hand. Because the fortunes of her family, indeed those of the whole clan, prospered at the time, Halima as well as other people assumed that it was the spirits' doing. In time, Halima came to be regarded as a blessing to her family, an asset to the whole clan. And she gloried in the special status her spirits gave her.

★ ★ ★

To the capital

It was because of her special powers that Halima was summoned to the capital. A big part of her clan was there. The most important and most powerful positions in the government were held by people of her clan. It had all started with one of their men, who had become very powerful in the government. He had called his relatives and found big government jobs for them. They in turn had called relatives of theirs till the government had virtually been taken over by Halima's people. And that had meant quick riches for everyone concerned. Nor had they been very scrupulous about getting what they wanted: anything that had stood in their way had been pushed aside or eliminated. At the time when Halima was summoned, her clan controlled the government and with that the wealth of the country so completely that no one dared to challenge them any more and they could get away with murder. Still they wanted to secure for themselves the extra protection of Halima's supernatural powers.

They had tried to get Halima's father to come to the capital as well. He was a man of stature, whose presence would have done honour to the clan. But he did not want to go. Old and resentful of change, he did not want to leave the peace and security of his village for the madness of the big city. But he was also afraid for his reputation. It was solid in his village but joining this gang might tarnish it, something he did not want to risk so near the end of his life. However, though he did not want to go himself, he had no reservations about sending his son and his daughters there. On one hand he hoped that they might get a slice of the big pie for themselves and so for the family. On the other hand he thought it would do no harm to have Halima there to protect the clan and to ensure its continued domination. Perhaps she could come to a deal with her spirits – she to continue looking after their infant and they to look after the welfare of the clan.

Halima did let herself be persuaded to go, but, before she went, she consulted her spirits. They asked her to perform two rituals. One was to prepare 'Tahleel', a special type of water, over which certain rituals were

Saida Hagi-Dirie Herzi

performed. People drank it or bathed in it to benefit from its powers. The second was to perform daily annual sacrifices to Gess Ade, the clan's twin spirit. Select parts of the innards of thousands of animals – hearts, kidneys, intestines and others – were to be offered to him every day on the eastern shore.

When Halima and her brother were ready to go, a cousin of theirs came from the big city to fetch them. From this cousin, who was an important government official, the two learned many things. They learned about the great privileges their people enjoyed in the city. They got an idea what wealth they had amassed since the clan had come 'to power'. They found out how completely the clan was in control of the government. They were awed, the more so when their informant told them that the clan had 'achieved' all this greatness in ten short years and that most of the people who now held important government positions were illiterate.

☆ ☆ ☆

In the big city
In the city, the two were given a beautiful villa complete with lots of servants and security guards. Within days, Halima's brother obtained an important government position of his own. He was made the head of the department that handled the sale of all incense, both inside and outside the country. Its official name was Government Incense Agency.

And Halima wasted no time carrying out the two requests of her spirits. She asked two things from the leaders of the clan. She asked them to bring all the water resources of the city together in one central pool to facilitate the performing of the 'Tahleel' and she requested the building of a huge slaughterhouse at the eastern shore. The leaders readily granted her requests since they were convinced that Halima's ministrations were of crucial importance for the continued success of the clan.

To centralise the city's water system, two huge water reservoirs were created, one in the eastern half and one in the western half of the city. Eventually all the wells of the city were destroyed, even the ones in private houses, and all water systems were connected to the two reservoirs. This way all the water consumed in the city came from the same source, and when Halima put the spell of her 'Tahleel' on the two reservoirs, it reached everyone.

One of the effects of the 'Tahleel' was to cure people of curiosity. Those who drank it stopped asking questions. Above all they stopped wondering about the actions of the clan's leading men. They became model subjects doing without question, without objection, what they were told to do. And Halima kept putting ever new spells on the water, faster than the old ones wore off. Though no one but she herself knew what kind of magic she put on the water, rumours abounded. One rumour had it that she performed certain incantations over the bath water of the leader and then released it into the reservoirs. There was no doubt in her mind and in the minds of the leaders that as long as everyone drank the water that carried her 'Tahleel' everything would go according to their plans.

When the new slaughterhouse went into operation, all other slaughterhouses were closed down. Unfortunately the new slaughterhouse was close to the Lido, the most popular of the city's beaches. In no time at all, the waters off the Lido swarmed with man-eating sharks, drawn there by the waste of blood and offals discharged by the slaughterhouse. After a number of people had been killed by the predators people stopped going to the Lido. There was no comment from the government. Quite obviously the slaughterhouse, where the sacrifices to Gess Ade were performed, was more important to the rulers of the country than the beach.

Every so often Halima would come to the slaughterhouse to check on the performance of the animal sacrifices. Here too she modified the rituals periodically to strengthen their effect.

As things kept going well for the tribe and her, Halima became more and more sure that she was the cause of it all. The clan's leaders too were convinced that they owed their continued success to Halima and her spirits. They heaped honours on her. They consulted her on all important issues and her counsel often proved invaluable. It was Halima, for instance, who thought up the idea of the shortages to keep the common people subdued. Shortages of all basic commodities were deliberately created and they kept people busy struggling for bare survival. They did not have time or energy to spare worrying about the goings-on in the government. The leaders of the clan felt more secure than ever.

Nearly twenty years have passed since Halima first went to the city. She is still performing her rituals, and the affairs of the clan are still prospering. Its men still hold all the important posts in the government and they still control the wealth of the country. As for the rest of the nation – they are mostly struggling to make ends meet, something that's becoming more and more difficult. And if there should be a few that might have time and energy left to start asking questions, Halima's 'Tahleel' and her various other forms of magic take care of them. The men of the clan continue to govern with the help of Halima's magic spell.

Revision questions
1. a) Give examples from the story to show that Halima and her people were superstitious.
   b) Do you believe in superstition?
2. Pick out any two statements that show people in Halima's community did not fully believe in Halima's powers.
3. What was the community's belief about twins?
4. Explain the two main reasons why Halima was summoned to the capital city.
5. a) Who formed the ruling class in the capital?
   b) Were they qualified?
   c) What does that tell you about the rulers?
6. a) What did Halima do just before she left for the capital?
   b) What two requests did she make of the leaders of her clan at the capital?
   c) Which of the requests was used to control and subdue the people?
   d) Do you support that kind of rule? Why or why not?
   e) How did the second request affect the welfare of the people?
7. a) In what way did Halima and her clan monopolise the economy of the country?
   b) What happened to the rest of the nation?
8. Give evidence to show that the rulers were aware of their misrule.

Topics for discussion
1. a) What do you understand by *Government by Magic Spell*?
   b) What is the danger of believing in superstitions?
2. With clear illustrations from the story, discuss the dominant themes in the story namely:
   a) misuse or abuse of power
   b) injustice
   c) nepotism
   d) corruption and greed.
3. How does the author use satire to poke fun at the misrule of Halima and her clan's government?
4. The saying 'power corrupts and absolute power corrupts absolutely' clearly applies to this story. Discuss.

Hama Tuma
Ethiopia

Hama Tuma is an Ethiopian writer and poet who has published several books in Amharic and English. His short story collection in English was published by Heinemann's African Writers Series (1993) under the title *The Case of the Socialist Witch Doctor & Other Stories*. Hama Tuma has also written two poetry books in English (*Of Spades and Ethiopians* and *Eating an American*), three in Amharic (*Habeshigna I and II, Gitm Wet Awke*) and an Amharic novel (*Kedadaw Chereka*). His latest collection of satirical short stories, *African Absurdities,* has also, been translated and published in French under the title *Afrique Politiquement Incorrent* by L'Harmattan, Paris (2001).

Who Cares for the New Millennium?

The hue and cry for the new millennium has left me cold and totally unmoved. As is always the case with Africans, I am forced to ask if it really is our millennium. Taking into account that most rural Africans would not even know a new year has come let alone a new millennium, and adding to these millions the Muslims who have their own calendar (and are not yet close to the twentieth century) and the Ethiopians, who also have their own old calendar and who would be seven years shy of 2000 when January comes, I dare to affirm that the so called millennium is not our affair.

Which does not mean we will not join the revelling if we could get the chance and the time out from the wars and the dreary struggle to survive. We Africans are condemned to repeat the past not because we forget it but mainly because we are forced to relive it. We repeat the tragedy as a tragedy and if there is any humour and joy in our life it is because we have stolen it or perhaps due to something in the African soul which makes us smile in the face of adversities and when everything and more goes wrong. This must be why well-to-do Africans from Abidjan to Addis Ababa, from Cairo to Pretoria are reserving rooms in those expensive Sheratons and Hiltons to celebrate the coming of the new millennium. It is comforting to note that at least our own bourgeoisie and rulers will enjoy the event just like the donors who bankroll them in the name of development and cooperation.

The new millennium will probably be a rerun of the B-grade life we Africans have been forced to endure in the one that is winding up. What makes the whole thing complicated is that words have now changed meaning and we do not know what is what. In the past millennium, we knew of the slave trade, we endured colonialism, we were subjected to neocolonialism and everybody said tribalism was bad and evil and this thing called 'ethnic' a backward concept, and national liberation struggles were fashionable. Come the new millennium, we are entering it as slaves but labelled free and independent. We are subjected to tyranny and foreign domination but we cannot utter the very word imperialism without risking being called an old guard, outmoded, archaic, a fossil. National liberation struggles seem to have died with Ché and nowadays the guerrillas are (check Sierra Leone and Uganda) worse than the government they are struggling against. Tribal and ethnic have now become kitsch and fad words; foods are ethnic, clothes are ethnic, ethnic is cool, *Tribal Jam* is the name of a musical group and does not refer to a traffic problem between warring tribes, and there are even governments who enjoy the support of the Western world while boldly proclaiming that they practise ethnic politics. So, who will fight? The enemy is dissimulated, hidden behind words, we are confused and in our confusion we are likely to welcome their millennium by fighting among ourselves. It is like 'the whole thing is complicated. Let me kill my neighbour' kind of reasoning. A Somali, Liberian and Rwandese logic you could say, to mention only a few. Maybe they will survive in the coming millennium while all others perish.

I am sure some people would accuse me of being a cynic, bleak in my vision if I even have one. Others could possibly say I am a reactionary with no 'we shall smash all the walls' revolutionary fervour. Perhaps they are all right but my problem is with this thing called our reality. My people say: a flower tree which is near a cactus will always weep. By nature or design, our continent is attached to the cactus (I do not want to call it Satan like the Iranians), it is forever weeping, bleeding. As I look back at the past century and observe that the new one our rulers are planning to celebrate with their masters finds us in the most depressing and disastrous condition, my optimism abandons me. I can tell you I am no wide-eyed True Believer or optimist but a Gramscian pretender with an 'optimism of the heart and the pessimism of the mind'. The most impoverished people? The highest infant mortality rate? The highest number of AIDS victims? The most number of refugees? The highest number of illiterates? The least developed countries? Ask any such question and the answer is Africa. Wouldn't it be better to claim that sometime in the past millennium they, whoever they may be, have conspired with our unelected leaders and stolen our next millennium and all the possibilities of our welcoming it with joy?

If the past and the present do not augur well for the future it does not mean, of course, that we Africans should not enjoy the celebration. Even those whose calendars do not say 2000 can still have a good time. Not for the ordinary reason of just enjoying themselves but to stand up to the callous rulers and power holders in the metropoles. We must go out and have a wild time to welcome in the new millennium just to

Who Cares for the New Millennium?

show to Bill Gates and the few other individuals who own more money than our continent can make in years, that they do not own the monopoly on joy and that poor as we are we have the right to party and enjoy ourselves. Celebrating the event should be our way of telling the IMF and all those claiming that they own our souls that we still gyrate and swoon to our own music and no one can steal our laughter even if they may hold us in debt.

But can we do it? Will, for example, Kabila and his enemies realise the importance of this particular event and let the people dance the new century in? I have my doubts. As I tried to explain something before, our rulers lack a sense of perspective and humour. They hate sharing joy. They will feast and party to welcome the millennium but they will for sure keep the prison gates locked and their soldiers out on the streets or in murderous operations. Our rulers are jealous of us, they want to see us famished and forlorn, bleeding and dying, suffering and groaning. In short, our rulers want us to live the new century like the past one. Some of us may thus be forced to become Muslims and postpone the coming of the new century. More optimistic ones could become Ethiopians and postpone the millennium for seven years. This may be the politics of the ostrich (hiding your head in the sand and imagining the danger has gone away) but in Africa it may be the only salvation for quite a few people, provided they are willing to change their religion and hoping that the Ethiopian government, which says there are no Ethiopians but ethnic groups living in a place called Ethiopia, could agree to accept that we call ourselves Ethiopians and get back to 1993.

It is so complicated this coming millennium. Should we ignore it? Should we acknowledge it and celebrate it so as to send messages to the industrialised countries? So many questions, so few answers: the perennial problem of Africa. Come January 2, 2000, tell me, if you will, if the new millennium has relieved us of the likes of Eyadema, Kabila, of famine and AIDS, of subservience to the West and of poverty, or if it even promises to do some of that and I will eat back all my bleak words and apologise and hail the new millennium with the fervour of a Bill Gates or of any African tyrant who had been hoping to continue to dance on our backs.

Revision questions
1 What is a millennium and which millennium is referred to in this story?
2 a) Which reasons show that due to cultural backgrounds Africans are not able to celebrate the new millennium at the same time?
   b) What is meant by 'seven years shy of 2000'?
3 Why are Africans said to live a 'B-grade' kind of life?
4 What problems faced by Africans are political in nature?

5 In what way does Hama Tuma suggest that Africans should celebrate the new millennium, if they have to? Do you agree with him?
6 Hama Tuma's story has no individual characters but character types we will call: the African, the African ruler, the Western masters. Describe the characteristics of each.
7 *Who cares for the new millennium* is a satirical title.
   a) What is satire?
   b) How does the author use it to bring out the problems that affect Africa?

Topics for discussion
1 Hama Tuma says that Africans started the second millennium as slaves and entered the third as slaves. How does he explain this?
2 'A flower tree which is near a cactus will always weep'. Using examples from the story, show how this is true of the Africa Hama Tuma presents.
3 The last paragraph summarises four major themes in the story. Identify and discuss each of them.
4 From your own knowledge, explain how the 'Let me kill my neighbour reasoning' affects Somalia, Liberia and Rwanda.

Wangui wa Goro
Kenya

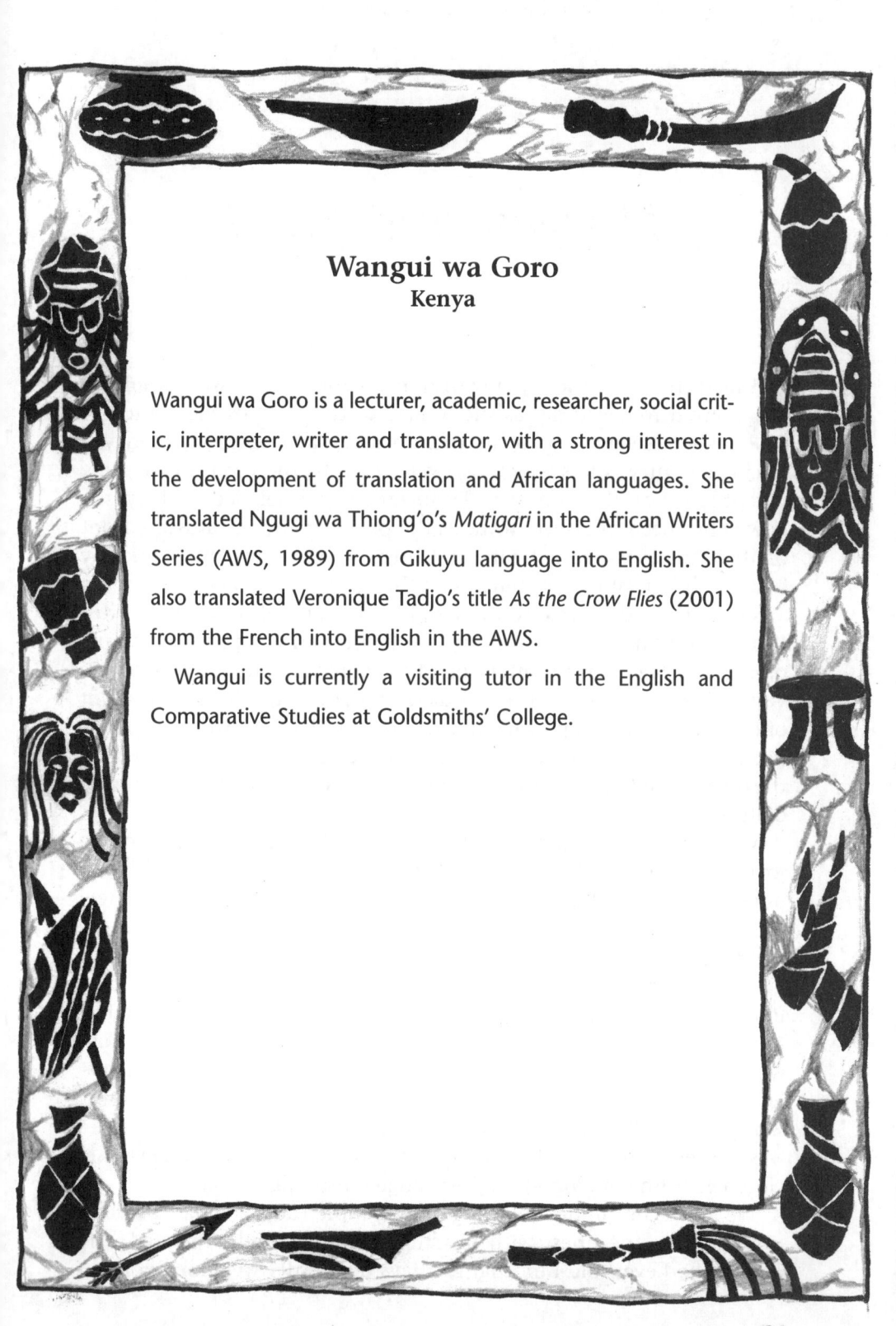

Wangui wa Goro is a lecturer, academic, researcher, social critic, interpreter, writer and translator, with a strong interest in the development of translation and African languages. She translated Ngugi wa Thiong'o's *Matigari* in the African Writers Series (AWS, 1989) from Gikuyu language into English. She also translated Veronique Tadjo's title *As the Crow Flies* (2001) from the French into English in the AWS.

Wangui is currently a visiting tutor in the English and Comparative Studies at Goldsmiths' College.

Heaven and Earth

She drifted into the room with nonchalant grace. A waft of talcum powder followed her as she walked to the front of the church. A predictable entry, or as her friend was to say later in her eulogy, a calculated entry. She shamelessly walked across the room to the only vacant space on the front pew. Deliberately, with feigned apology, she bowed her head in respect towards the preacher and towards the front of the church where a figure of Christ on the cross hung midway between the front of the church and the ceiling.

She wore a bright yellow and red dress with floral patterns that rustled as she walked to the front of the church and settled herself amply on the pew. She drew the attention of the bored congregation who were very relieved to seize on the spectacle before them, inhaling the scent of the Yardley talcum powder mixed with familiar fresh womanly musk mixed with some fake perfume from abroad. They were all relieved by the distraction that presented itself in what was otherwise a patronising diatribe.

Mme Lady ceremoniously settled her wide hips on the pew, smiling jovially at the neighbours, greeting others, waving at others in an unconscious, unselfish and most unapologetic manner, completely oblivious of the commotion that her whole entry had generated at the Sunday morning service.

'And women, you shall adorn yourself for your husbands,' the vicar found himself saying with a certain level of annoyance at the effect Mme Lady's presence was having on the attention of the congregation, which he had believed he was, until now, sort of enjoying. He shamelessly cast a glaring look towards her. As if to annoy him further Mme wriggled herself in the pew further, and the loud rustle of the clothes was now even more audible all the way down the church hall due to her closeness to the microphones. Her bangles also jingled loudly.

She loved the Sunday morning drama, Mme Lady. She had a certain contempt for the priest with his stupid sermons and wondered why nobody had ever told him that the days of chastity were long gone (if ever they had been). What the Church really needed to do was focus upon how to educate the youth on restraint, not so much for moral reasons but more so for reasons of health. In her mind she began planning a condom distribution centre, as well as HIV/AIDS counselling sessions. She took her handkerchief from between her breasts and wiped her brow. The bangles jingled noisily again, much to the vicar's consternation. He was clearly in competition and banged the pulpit, trying to win back the attention of his congregation. Mme Lady loved this weekly tussle with the vicar. He was a short rotund figure. She had no time for him when he timed his pastoral visits perfectly to coincide with mealtimes, not just in her case but also in the case of other well-to-do women. Now, Mme Lady, she had sussed him out a long time ago. Each time she saw him coming through the gate and approach her house, the food would be stashed away from sight with lightning speed and everybody would suddenly find they were very busy. Not that they were lacking in generosity, but they believed that people had to behave themselves according to visiting etiquette and should wait to be invited for meals. This of course was not the traditional approach, but in this modern day and age people were too busy and did not have time to keep going back and forth to the kitchen when whoever decided to drop in at whatever time. Mme Lady used to prepare the food in her house at her husband's request. Nobody else was allowed into the kitchen other than to clean it. Mme Lady would often greet the preacher warmly. 'How hot you look,' she would begin and meet him cheerily with a glass of cold water from the ceramic cooling urn, which stood in the middle of the living room, although she had a freezer and ice.

After the usual pleasantries, she would guide him towards the door telling him how busy she was with this and that and the other. She would take him into the garden and point out the weeds, which suddenly needed plucking, or digging, no matter what time of day it was. The subtlety did not escape him and he would soon realise that he needed to take his culinary interest elsewhere. Most times, he ended up with a meal from one of the peasant women who felt sorry for him because he had no wife, and who thought that men should not cook.

Mme Lady's bangles jingled as she took her handkerchief from between her breasts again. It was so hot. Why did all these people come to church anyway? They were poor peasant women mainly. Their heads were clad with pretty, patterned scarves that they used to cover their hair, hair which she had never seen at any time. She now imagined what wonders of beauty lay hidden beneath those headscarves. She felt tempted to knock them off accidentally and began scanning the congregation for her first likely victim. She could tell by their very attentiveness that they believed everything that the preacher was saying to be gospel truth. She wondered where their husbands were, and who was looking after the children. True, some of the children were at Sunday school, but where were the older ones? Up to what mischief were they getting? If she had teenage children, she would require them to come to church with her or she would stay at home and look after them. In these days, you couldn't afford to take any chances. Mme Lady continued to admire the pretty, pressed cotton dresses and buttoned cardigans. She felt a laugh of compassion for this situation and anger at their exploitation particularly by the vicar who loved to preach hell and brimstone whenever the collection needed boosting. She knew all these women well. They had at one time or another come to her for assistance on this or that matter which sometimes involved domestic problems, sometimes their health, sometimes finances and because of this she had become the central point of the community. She loved this.

She had been born in this semi-urban community where she had also grown up. She had gone to town to seek a fortune but her future husband, known as Kim, had gone to seek her and brought her back to the community by marrying her and then establishing her as the First Lady, so to speak. He told everybody how much he loved her and that there could be no other woman in the world for him but her.

She was indeed a very beautiful woman in stature. She was not very tall, nor was she very fat, but she was amply built. She enhanced her skin with skin lighteners, although she was always on the verge of stopping as she heard that they caused skin cancer, and she did not want to die.

As Mme Lady continued to contemplate the upturned faces of the congregation from where she sat on the sideways facing pew, she could not help herself from feeling blessed at being so lucky.

She hissed involuntarily as the thoughts of the problems that the women faced crossed her mind, and the facile nature of how simplistic the priest's sermons could sometimes be. Yet she had first hand knowledge of their lives. She recognised the fact that the church doubled up as a focal point of the community and that many good things happened there socially. The vicar stopped mid-sentence with incredulity on hearing her hiss. How dare she challenge him before this congregation? Mme Lady was quite unaware of the distraction her commotion and behaviour were causing. She had now started flossing her teeth with a toothpick, her one arm comfortably tucked under her bosom. The vicar now, in deliberate fashion, resumed his sermon, calculating the delivery of each word and punching it through the air, his short fingers now clenched into a fist which he waved in Mme Lady's direction. Mme Lady sensed the coming onslaught and suddenly became aware of her surroundings again.

'God designated the role of men and women in the community clearly. In the Bible, God, from the very beginning, clearly created man in his own image and gave him woman to be his helper. This is stressed throughout the Bible. Women should obey their husbands and remain humble till the end of their days. Men and women each have areas of responsibility designated by their biology'.

'If only it were so simple,' Mme Lady thought to herself, knowing as she did the difficulties that face women in their lives, not just in this community but nationally and maybe even worldwide. She wondered what kind of world such a man came from and what motivated him: whether it was just real belief, or a desire to patronise women, of whom he couldn't have had very much experience unless there was something he was not telling. She had heard stories of wily vicars and priests who would visit women during the daytime and relieve them not only of their burdens and food, but their money and more.

Soon, the sermon ended and to everyone's relief it was time for the collection and the final hymn, which Mme Lady sang as loudly as ever with her usual gusto. You could hear her voice and deliberate intonation above everybody else's over the loudspeaker. Everybody knew that she had her own designated seat, and nobody dared sit on it even if it was the only space left in the church and she was not present. They knew that she would roll up eventually.

At last everyone rushed outside to the bright sunshine with sheer relief that their duty was now done and they could get back home to the usual chores. Once outside the women gathered around Mme Lady, again filling the preacher with consternation as he stood at the door waiting to greet his congregation and find out how they were faring. Several women and children walked up to Mme Lady just to greet her or be part of the entourage that stood around her. Mme Lady laughed happily, shaking hands, listening attentively and loving the feeling of being useful, valued and wanted. Mme Lady was one of those women you could not ignore in any crowd. She was typical of any group dynamic; flamboyant, loud, and the type who seem unabashed by anything.

Soon Mme Lady's husband turned up in his big Mercedes-Benz to pick her up from the church. He came out of the car and greeted the vicar apologising for not having attended the service but promising that he would do so the following Sunday.

That was going to be an interesting week, the vicar said, because it would be Father's Day. The church would be addressing the role of the family, and the women would have an opportunity to speak at this occasion to give their views on fatherhood, the celebration of fatherhood and the role that men could play in their lives and those of their children, particularly the male ones. It would be an occasion of thanksgiving that this community had yielded such wonderful fathers.

This service was one of the best attended by men. It was also well attended by several women – they were not going to miss the occasion of seeing these men. These were the men they rarely saw, as some of them lived in the city now and they only appeared on rare occasions such as Christmas and baptisms or funerals unless there was another very special occasion at the church.

Mme Lady rushed to a meeting with the women to finalise and sort the finer points that needed to be made for the preparation. The celebrations were always held communally on the green in front of the church on such occasions. The women were required to volunteer their services to ensure a success. Mme Lady was always the leading light in the arrangement of these affairs and she needed to remind some of the women of their responsibilities and make sure that all of the little last minute issues had been ironed out.

Afterwards, Mme Lady got into the front of her husband's car, waving her handkerchief to cool herself down, happy that she had performed her Sunday duties. She looked forward to having some repose from the afternoon heat after lunch, but even now she knew that they were going to have guests. Undoubtedly this would be at lunchtime and she would not be able to rest until well after nine o'clock when the last guests had gone. On Sundays she was more flexible and friends, relatives and acquaintances knew they could visit her, unannounced or uninvited. For this reason she made sure that the cook prepared extra food. Even the vicar would be welcome on a Sunday as long as he did not overstay his welcome or mingle inappropriately with their other guests. Besides, it was her day to be a good wife to her husband, by entertaining his friends and mates.

True to form, they found one of their urban friends' BMW parked in the driveway, and the man of the family standing outside the car, waving his keys impatiently. He was waiting to see Mme's husband, who was a businessman, and naturally his wife had come along with him and the children who were sitting in the back of the car. They must have been coming from their church in the city which normally started and finished earlier.

The following Sunday the church was fully packed. The vicar wore his best scarf and he made sure that his gown was especially well-ironed. He had prepared the sermon of sermons which would bring the doubters back to church and bolster the community and the church coffers, which were dwindling considerably with the massive male exodus.

He was even ready for Mme Lady, whom he would give the opportunity to settle down. Today he would remain calm. It was a men's day, and he felt truly blessed to be celebrating with so many fathers, their responsibility to their families and to society. He had prepared the sermon carefully, and was continuing with the previous week's theme on the place of responsibility in the family. Today he would tackle the role of men and round up on the importance of godliness which was the guide to good fatherhood and husband-hood. There were too many single parents nowadays, and too many men failing in their obligations – even if they were sometimes driven into temptation by the devil.

By the time he was half-way through the sermon Mme Lady had not as yet made an appearance. This was not unusual, and anyway he knew that she was busy organising the reception that would be hosted after the service.

He continued with the sermon steadily driving towards the climax and increasing the tempo of his voice as he headed there. He was disappointed that Mme Lady was not in her place for this delivery. She always gave him a good run for his delivery, timing himself and his pitch to her interruptions which, although they irritated him, had now become a feature of the Sunday service. He was not the only one who noticed her absence, and the congregation suffered the better-than-usual sermon that was now being rained upon them.

After the service, the preacher disrobed hurriedly, as on this occasion he would have a better opportunity to mingle with his flock at the coming reception. He was to make a further speech there, urging the young men to remain committed to the community which had given them their start and yielded their success. He had some envelopes to encourage them to support the church and standing order forms to enable them to continue giving generously. On these occasions the collections were usually quite good, motivated perhaps by guilt, and the preacher did not hesitate in rubbing this in.

He had seen Mme Lady's husband in the congregation and went out to the crowds gathered outside the church to see if he could catch him. He was nowhere to be seen and as the vicar came round the corner, he believed that he saw the distinctive metallic grey Mercedes speeding away.

He went to the hall kitchen to see if Mme Lady was there, but she was not. He asked the women if they had seen her. They seemed lost and aimless without her. Somebody suggested politely that maybe he should go and see whether she was coming, as they still needed the napkins and cutlery, which she had said she would bring.

He asked one of the young men, a doctor named Vim, to drive him to Mme Lady's house which was not too far away. His little old car would not start easily, and, in any case, it was blocked in by all the big modern cars which belonged to today's unique congregation. He had no heart to drive his old car out of this place on a day like this.

They got to Mme Lady's compound which appeared isolated. Normally it was bustling with life, but today there was an eerie lifelessness about it. But at this time on a Sunday, it would be, he justified to himself, as everybody was at church.

He decided to knock anyway, to see if there was anyone in. He would leave a message and collect the cutlery and napkins and head back to the church – that is if the maid was in, but he was aware that this was her day off and it would be unusual for her to be there. He knocked again and thought that he heard slow footsteps inside, and then the door opened tentatively and there was Mme Lady, wearing a blood-stained gown, her eyes sealed by enormous swellings around them.

'What happened to you?' he exclaimed involuntarily, in a high-pitched voice. Mme Lady had dark welts and blotches across her face and traces of dried blood down her cheeks.

'Were you burgled or something?'

'No, who is it anyway?'

'It's Sam, the preacher.'

'Oh, I thought it was my husband returning from the church,' she said, full of embarrassment. 'I am afraid I cannot see you. Maybe you should come back another time,' she said with a sob in her voice and she started to close the door.

The preacher could not believe what he was seeing. He felt overcome. He had never seen anything like this in his life.

'Did they steal anything? What did they want?' he continued to ask in a shrill voice.

'Nothing,' she said, and pushed the door further, trying to close it.

The preacher, who had now forgotten the original purpose for his visit, stopped her. At heart he truly liked Mme Lady and he was not going to leave her in this state.

'Come with me, Vim is in the car; we will take you to hospital.'

He called to the young doctor, 'Vim, here, hurry, Mme Lady has been attacked by thugs, look.'

Vim hurriedly came round to support Mme Lady who walked out of the house, leaving the door ajar.

'What happened, Mama? What happened to you, can you speak? I will rush you to my hospital, although I am not on duty today; they will be able to see you quite quickly, and as it is a Sunday, it should be quiet.'

When they got to the hospital, Vim decided to stay with Mme Lady and urged the vicar to take his car and hurry back to his congregation. He had known Mme Lady all his life, and had admired her as he grew up. But she was way out of his league, being the legendary beauty that she was, and, anyway, nobody crossed Kimanja's path.

'Who hit you?' he asked gently. He did not need an answer. He knew and looked sadly at this beautiful woman, now denied sight by the swellings that covered her eyes. He had seen this kind of incident frequently enough, but could not believe that a woman of her stature, with her power, money or standing could be a victim of it. He also knew that she would not say.

'You can talk to me, the vicar is gone now. Was it Kimanja? How long has it been going on?'

The doctors treated her, and within a week she was feeling much better. She convinced Vim not to tell anybody, not even the vicar who visited her frequently and prayed fervently for her, as if she was about to die.

Her husband did not visit her once, but the women from the congregation came with their various offerings of food and fruit. Although the hospital was a fair way away, they made a great effort, leaving their weekly chores to show their respect for her.

'You are not going back there?' Vim asked her on her last day, 'Are you?'

'Where else can I go? I have no money and in our community you know that women are dependent on their husbands. My family will not take me back; a very high dowry was paid for me which they cannot repay.'

'Surely you know better than that! You will tell them the truth.'

'No one will believe me and even if they do, they will blame me. They think I am spoilt and that it is my fault! I have no qualifications and I cannot find a job at this age. I don't even have children, as I am barren. He is everything to me. What about my reputation and his? Everyone looks up to me.'

'What is your reputation compared to your life? There is a way, there must be. Don't go yet, I will talk to a nurse here who co-ordinates a domestic violence project.'

'You must not tell anybody about this; besides, I have been discharged and I have to go home.'

'At least wait and let me get you this woman's contact. I will also drive you home.'

'No, you can't do that, it will only make matters worse for me.'

The following Sunday, Mme Lady was the first in church. She was wearing dark glasses to hide the swellings round her eyes. She had to keep up appearances, otherwise people would start talking. She was so grateful for this little community which had shown her compassion and made her feel valued.

She had not seen her husband since she returned from hospital. She sat throughout the service with her head bowed in contemplation. What could she do? It was not right that she, the cornerstone of the community, was in such a situation.

'We saw last week how the men have continued to sustain their homes and how we in our community are blessed with wonderful men who care about their families.'

'If only it were so simple,' Mme Lady whispered to herself. Domestic violence, eh? How many women here were victims of this? And how had she arrived in this position?

Tears began rolling down her face, as she clutched the piece of paper that Vim had given her, and she stood to leave the congregation, resolved to go and seek help from the nurse.

The bright sunlight hit her eyes, and although she was wearing dark glasses, she felt her eyes sting sharply.

'Where do you think you are going?' she heard the familiar voice ask her angrily. 'Where have you been all week?' The fear welled up and she felt the urge to scream.

She heard a faint voice coming from her throat saying that she had been to hospital and had not been home before coming to the church.

'Liar,' he said, and struck her heavily across her face.

She screamed loudly and several members of the congregation came rushing out to see what was going on. They found Mme Lady on her knees on the ground holding her head, with tears and blood running down her face. Kim walked off angrily and the vicar took her back to the vestry. He urged the congregation to go home while he took Mme Lady back to the hospital.

'Is that what happened to you last Sunday?' he asked, now ashamed of the thoughts he had had against this and other women, and ashamed at some of the sermons he had preached.

'Can you please call Vim, or take me to him,' Mme Lady said resolutely, in a voice the vicar had never heard before.

'Of course, of course.'

'And next time when you preach those sermons, remember that you are condemning so many women, like me, to suffering at the hands of men. We come to church as a sanctuary, a safe place, the only place we are allowed to go to without supervision, and you see, he even comes to pick me up from there although I can drive and have my own car. You should live in the real world! You have never been married and you do not know what it is like for us women, we have nowhere to go!' She spoke with a trembling in her voice, surprising herself with the candour of her outburst, when she was usually politely tolerant.

The doctor seemed to be expecting them, as he came out of his house

Wangui wa Goro

promptly to meet them once he saw the vicar's car drawing up at his gate.

'She can stay with me for the time being, I have a big house. I will go and call one of the nurses to stay with us so she can feel safe. You must promise not to tell anyone where she is, until we have found a solution for her.'

The vicar drove away sadly, preparing the following week's sermon in his head.

He felt upset that he would not be seeing Mme Lady for a while, and that he had failed in his duty by not recognising her as an ordinary broken woman who wore a façade out of fear. He felt ashamed of the community, yet battled with God's will. He could not condone her leaving her husband, no matter what the circumstances. Yet he had been shocked beyond words when he saw Mme Lady's eyes sealed by the beatings. Should she stay and be killed? Were there exceptional circumstances in which divorce and separation could be tolerated? He thought of Mandela and other people who had divorced their wives and began to think that perhaps it was time the church and society began to think differently about these issues. It was not going to be an easy sermon, but he would pray for guidance, pray for Mme Lady, pray for the congregation, pray for Kimanja for he too was a human being who needed God's blessing. He had a week in which to resolve the dilemmas that were torturing his soul and turning in his head.

Revision questions
1. a) Describe Mme Lady's appearance and mannerisms on the first day you meet her in church.
   b) Attempt an explanation as to why you think she is called Mme Lady.
2. a) Describe Mme Lady's character:
      i) The first time you meet her
      ii) The second time you meet her.
      Would you agree that she is one and the same person?
   b) Why do you think she seems to have a double personality?
3. a) What is Mme Lady's opinion about HIV/AIDS?
   b) Do you agree with her?
4. a) Does Mme Lady strike you as genuinely religious?
   b) Why was she so keen on going to church?
5. a) Discuss the use of suspense in this story.
   b) What hints are you given for the turn of events as they unfold in the story? Are the hints convincing?
6. a) Would you agree that the vicar was naïve?
   b) Who is wiser, the vicar or Dr Vim?

7 Why did Mme Lady find it difficult to leave her husband?
8 Not much is said about Kimanja, Mme Lady's husband. From what you hear and see of him, reconstruct his character.

Topics for discussion
1 In creating Mme Lady's character, the author fails to convince us that the lady was just 'an ordinary broken woman who wore a façade out of fear' especially in the way she treats the vicar. Do you agree?
2 This is a story about 'domestic violence'.
   a) What do you know about domestic violence?
   b) Who are the most disadvantaged in cases of domestic violence. Why?
   c) Suggest ways in which it can be minimised or eliminated in society.
3 Discuss the relationships between:
   a) husbands and wives
   b) the vicar and his congregation
   c) Mme Lady and the other women.

Kyalo Mativo
Kenya

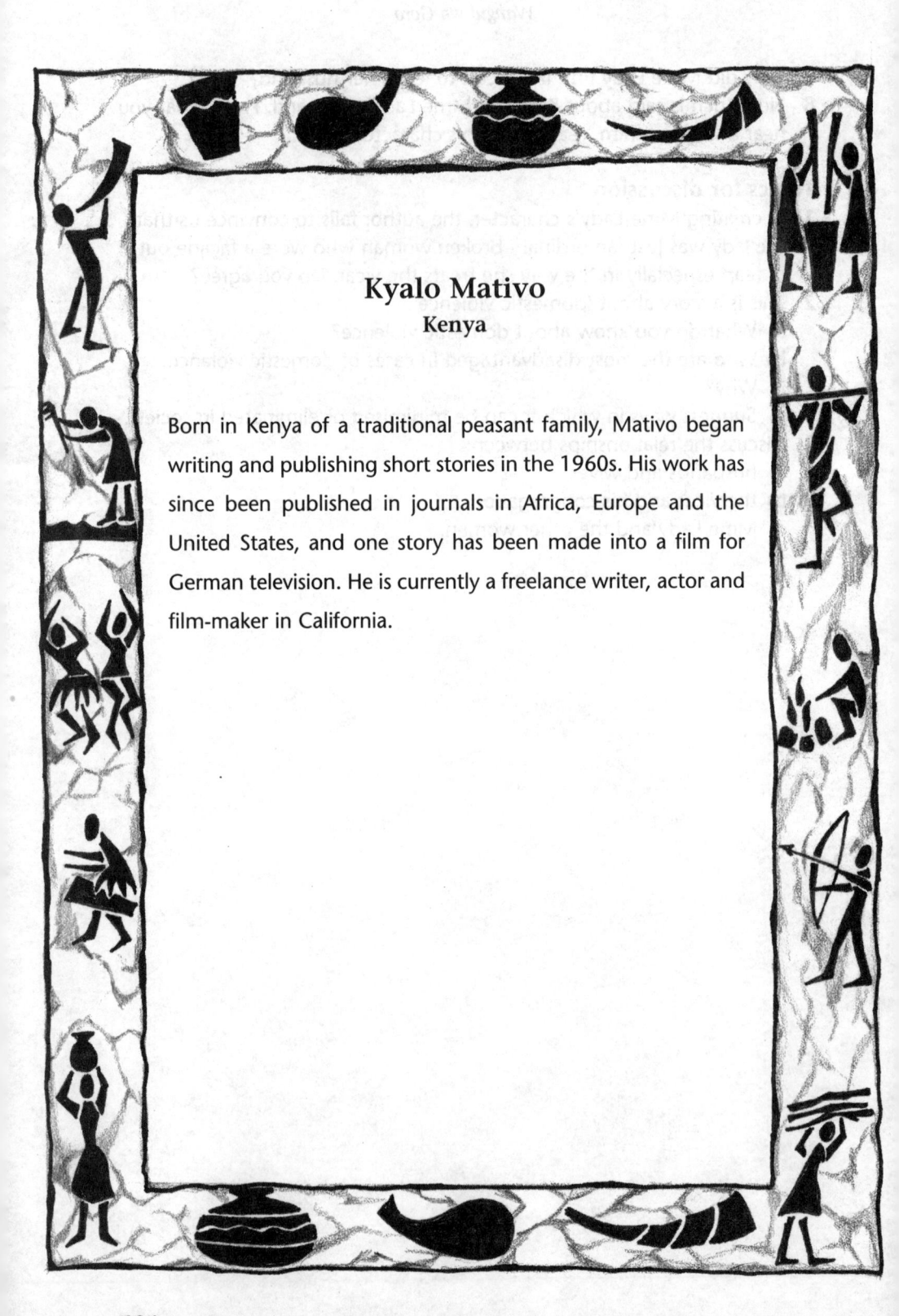

Born in Kenya of a traditional peasant family, Mativo began writing and publishing short stories in the 1960s. His work has since been published in journals in Africa, Europe and the United States, and one story has been made into a film for German television. He is currently a freelance writer, actor and film-maker in California.

On the Market Day

Kamali Lango woke up in the midst of the night, long before the village owl. Kokia, his wife, was already up and his food was ready: a maize meal – yesterday's left-overs – which was re-warmed in boiling water, a cup of grade-two hot coffee with a touch of powdered milk, and sour milk. He ate with relish.

He ate to a powerful munching silence. The open-air kerosene can-lamp, fondly baptised *Shike-n'tandike*, flapped its flame noisily as if in a concerted effort to break the uncomfortable silence, and the embers on the hearth cracked in positive response. It was a familiar cracking.

One of the young ones stirred, and the parents froze. The father stopped chewing, and the mother held her breath ... If only there was a way of destroying that dangerous smell of food ... But the young one merely turned on his other side and fell back into sleep. That was all.

'Remember, my mother is coming here the day after the day after tomorrow,' Kokia said almost in a whisper. There was no immediate answer; he knew only too well what was on the agenda. But he had to respond in one way or another.

'Yes, I know.'
'What should I do then?'
'I intend to be back by then.'
'And if not?'

The wife was not given to prying. But in trying times vagueness is a crime.

'The day after the day after tomorrow is not yet here,' he said defensively. 'There is no cause for hysteria,' he continued. 'We are not yet trashed; so we can still find a way out. Have you joined those hopeless people who go around shouting, "we shall not survive, we shall not survive, this is the end of the tether ... this is the ..."?' The words threatened to choke in his throat. And an obstinate sonorous echo continued to ring in his mind like an alarm clock: '... is the end of the tether ... the end of the tether ... end of the tether ... of the tether ...'.

It was indeed the end of the tether. At least as far as that unpleasant conversation was concerned. So he stood up, picked up his wrapped-up blanket, his stick, his small torch, and stepped out into the dark and silent night. From across the Wingoo Valley, the faint and lonely wailing of a dog came riding the air current.

After a reflective interval, the mother lifted up the can-lamp and held it above her head as she bent to survey the young ones. Then she put out the flame and went back to sleep.

All that was routine. Last week she did the same. The week before last, she did the same. Last year, when she had only seven children, it was the same thing. And at the end of the year, when her ninth child begins to walk, she will do it again.

The man was counting his fingers as he groped his way through the dark. Well, he knew his way quite well, he has walked the same path for ... now let's see ... three ... four? No, five years at least. Somehow, even during the darkest of the nights he managed to find his way. 'The sun always rises, even if not always to the Glory of God.' That was his magic wand, his consolation. But a consolation.

Last year, he reckoned, he made, ooh, let's see ... eh ... about ... one ... or ... Yes, one hundred shillings net. He lost how many cattle? ... The spotted one, the sharp-horned heifer, the brown bull, the white-crowned cow, the black-topped ... the ... that's all. Or? Yes, that's all. Nevertheless ... Nevertheless, the sun always rises 'even if not always to the Glory of God'. This year, if all goes well, 'I mean if the rains fall ...' he paused for a while to wrestle with an agonising memory. 'There used to be a thick forest here, saturated with life ... and now all that remains is a dry whirlwind ... Anyway this year if the rains come I could make as much as, ooh, two hundred, three hundred ...' But he stopped there. There was this disturbing memory, you see, that for the last two years, if he could remember well – and it was a curse to have to remember – there had been no rain, not even an imitation of it. And two or three days ago Radio Wananchi reminded the people that lack of rain, and therefore famine, are natural phenomena against which man is powerless. It added: 'Let that be known to those who are accusing the government of doing nothing; let them know that their rumour-mongering will not be tolerated.'

Kamali Lango had bought himself a transistor radio two ... three rainy seasons ago to keep abreast with the times. And that night after the message had been relayed to the people, the peasants echoed it back and forth in the usual manner, nodding their heads to the truth of the broadcast and beating their breasts cursing the harsh, invisible and uncontrollable power so magnificently blamed by the broadcast: nature. Naturally it was their fault for failing to come together to gather the necessary money for a water project. Every fool knew it. But one thing was clear: the weather broadcasts had long ceased to bear the summarised forecasts of cold spells and low clouds. They had long turned into out-and-out political commentaries exonerating the government of the people, freely chosen in the most becoming and the latest democratic fashion in the world.

Down the footpath the man had gone quite a distance by now. The first glimmer of light found him still tramping; but not alone. After every other kilometre or so he met a line of villagers from beyond the mountain marching their donkeys in the opposite direction to fetch drinking-water. It was known that these villagers spent four days to accomplish that mission. And the old ones say it was the first time they had known that to happen. Ah well, it was rumour-mongering. But then so what? As the famous broadcast so aptly put it, 'you don't expect things to fall down like manna.'

'Greetings!'
'How do you fare?'
'Well. Only you.'
'And the people.'
The people – Hmm, sorry – the people are well too.
Day-break.

The naked sun rose slowly and surely, an accursed red ball of ill-will. For days on end, it had risen in the same manner behind the same mountain. Sure enough, another day-break. And there, all around him, rose a sea of dust, stretching far and beyond the sky-line. It was a familiar sight and the man had long ceased to take note of it. His feet, covered with red soil, carried him triumphantly as they had always done countless times before. He cocked up his head on one side and sent a couple of bullets of spittle hurtling through the air. There was still enough saliva left all right. And when the times are good, a morning like this welcomes him like a ruling monarch; yes, it washes his feet with dew, and the clean air cleanses his foul breath. He shook his head as if to rid himself of an unpleasant thought. It was then, when he lifted his head, that he found out that actually he no longer had the monopoly of the path. He was walking ahead of and behind an ever-growing line of other people, all like him trying to beat the deadline of the tyrannical sun. The line of the people grew longer and longer, and soon there was a steady flow of men and women. Now the path was a sprightly scene of dust from which silence was banished. A spontaneous murmur came into being, changing slowly into a buzz. Jingles joined, and out of this combination a rhythm was born. There was chanting and whistling. The songleader was a fly-whisk-wielding home-made poet in his own right. He marched in the very front of the line and dished out doses of the countryside's pride, and the men joined in at the prescribed intervals while the women provided the chorus. The current song was in praise of a young man who had collected all kinds of degrees from all over the world, but who returned to his native home on foot. White civilisation had failed to annex him. He had come home to serve the people in any capacity they would assign to him. The circumstances of this young man's beautiful history were once again unfolded in the song, and all natural elements bore witness to them:

LEADER
When the moon shines
It is because Mbula is out there
Visiting the people;

When the wind blows
It is because Mbula
Is there caring for the sick;

When the sun rises
It is because Mbula
Rose up early to attend to the young;

So what do you say?

CHORUS
We have heard his footsteps
Shuffling among the reeds
And on the countryside on rainy days
We have seen his deeds;

And we have felt his tears
Trickling on our cheeks:

ALL
And he will feed the hungry
For he is the son of the country.

It was high season. Everybody knew what that meant. Even Kamali Lango couldn't quite plead innocent of it. Events were galloping to a head in the muddy arena of politics. And so was this procession. And so was the heat of the sun. And shortly they would be there.

Pancreas Mbula was already there. Unlike his opponents, he was the first to arrive. A few other people had already arrived too, but serious business hadn't begun until the group had been reinforced by the new recruits. Then he stood up and spoke about the main points of his programme: free education, free medicine, provision of irrigation projects and establishment of clinics and nursery schools in the villages where the people lived.

'But,' he went on, 'there is no substitute for self-help. We have to start somewhere, and the main force will come from you. On my part, I shall do, as I have always done, what I can to contribute to a fair social set-up. I shall persuade the government to allocate some money to these projects. I pledge myself and promise, as sure as I stand here now, to serve you with all my heart. Indeed I'm aware of what the previous Member of Parliament did during the term of his office; he abused the privilege you bestowed on him, and instead of representing you, he represented himself, his family and his close circle of friends. Ten years ago he entered the Parliament as poor as a butterfly, but ten years later he left it a fat maggot of a millionaire. And that is not all: he has the shamelessness to campaign for another term of office!'

A thunderous applause.

'I say it again as I have done several times before: the real power rests with you. Your votes are too precious to give away to a bloodsucking parasite. Let it be your choice that I be the next MP for Ngangani, and I tell you, before the end of two years, you yourselves will be the witnesses of change. If in two years no changes have occurred, then you have the right to come and say so to my face. I will deserve to be removed without hesitation.'

'What will you do about the lack of rain, son?' the tired voice of a widower demanded from the crowd.

'Well,' he cleared his throat, 'you have all heard the story on the radio about the lack of rain being a natural catastrophe. Right now, we are sitting on a pool of water, and on both sides we are flanked by two perennial rivers. Lift up your eyes,' he said, pointing away, 'do you all see that mountain towering about the clouds with a white cap on top of it? Well, that "cap" is actually a frozen lake whose water melts four times every year and trickles down the mountain-sides right through the thick forest surrounding it, zigzagging its way down the slopes. That melted water is equal to twice as much water again as we receive from natural rain. Indeed with that much water we can turn this semi-desert into a green field all year round. And we have the will and the energy for that ...'

Another applause went out from the crowd.

'Whoever doubts that, doubts the power of the people ...'

Another applause.

'... And I'm asking only to be blessed with your votes, your valuable votes, in order to make this dream a reality.'

The ecstatic crowd broke into the chant:

We have heard his footsteps
Shuffling among the weeds,
And on the countryside on rainy days
We have seen his deeds;
And we have felt his tears
Trickling on our cheeks:
And he will feed the hungry
For he is the son of the country.

For Kamali Lango it was a familiar event processed in a familiar manner. He had seen and heard it all before and, like all others, had waited for the promised changes, and was still waiting. He left the scene of political action and continued on his journey.

It was now midday.

The market place was bursting with pompous peasant pride, a splendid scene of swarming flies, scorching sun, mooing cows and bellowing bulls. And from time to time, in the midst of this motley of noise, a sharp cry of agony would be heard. It was the cry of a baby demanding what in the circumstances was a simple impossibility: food. He walked right through the market from the western to the eastern section of it, until he arrived at the most familiar of all the familiar scenes: the cattle shed.

The auction was already in full swing. The smell of dung, the ceaseless mooing of the cattle, the yelling of the merchants and the boiling earth, all added to the atmosphere of cut-throat competition which brought the men into a beard-to-beard confrontation. And wielding your dagger, you stabbed and got stabbed, for it was the nature of the trade.

'There goes a majestic family bull ... Look how he strides; what a public show of strength.' It was the auction master announcing the next candidate for raucous bidding.

'Two hundred,' shouted a prospective buyer.

'Two hundred,' repeated the auction master.

'Two hundred and fifty,' came a challenging voice.

'Two hundred and fifty ... two hundred and fifty ...'

'Three hundred,' yet another bidder.

'Four hundred.'

'Four hundred ... four hundred ... four hundred. The purchase has been made,' concluded the auction master.

Kamali Lango meditated for a while. He wasn't sure any more now whether he could participate in the bidding without running a risk. But then that's exactly what the thing amounted to: risk. Meanwhile another bull was put up.

'... A healthy animal of beefy elegance,' the master eulogised.

'Three hundred ... three hundred...'

'Four hundred ... four hundred...'

'Five hundred ... five hundred ... five ...'

'Six hundred,' a billy-goat-like voice pierced the air with a malicious intent. That was Menge. The audience let out a murmur of indifference. The new bidder was the renowned local cattle-dealer, rumoured to possess the capability to sweep out all the cattle in stock within and outside the community at any given moment. In matters of trade, his word was final. Everybody knew it. But as a matter of formality, the auction master proceeded to make the count-down. And as he did so, a wiry, wind-blown weakling climbed down the buyers' platform and wound his way to the centre of the bargaining shed. Aware of his financial power, Menge began to drive the animal out of the shed long before the count-down was over.

'*Seven hundred!*'

It wasn't just the noise which startled some people, sent others choking with laughter and left others numb. It was simply the unexpected turn of events. It was so devastating that Menge's stick fell down from his hand. He stood still for a moment like one who had been shot in the back with an arrow, then picked up his stick and walked back to the buyers' platform. He needed simply to shout 'one thousand' to silence every prospective challenger. But he wasn't going to accept a challenge from a nondescript peasant. No, he dismissed the challenge with contempt. Meanwhile the auction master had finished the count, and like a skilful hunter that he felt himself to be at this moment, Kamali Lango stepped down and marched proudly to collect his prey. All watched him walk across the bargaining shed as he drove his new deal out.

Then he went to the cashier's desk and counted seven hundred shillings from his pocket. It was all he had.

Seven hundred shillings was his life-savings, his working capital for five years. Now that it had changed into a four-legged commodity for self-expansion, he ought to get added value of ... ooh, ... one ... two hundred shillings? Who knows? Maybe more, maybe less. But he didn't need to worry about that; it wasn't the first time it had happened to him. Now, as before, there was always the rising sun.

Twilight.

That night, as always, Kamali Lango stayed with a friend of his who lived mid-way between the buying and the selling market. By sunset the next day he would go to the selling market. After selling his bull, he

Kyalo Mativo

planned to catch a bus leaving for his home that evening. But he would get off at Kaimu market to buy two sacks of maize and then wait for the midnight bus from the coast. He would load his two sacks of maize in it and travel to Kamulamba, the country-bus station nearest to his home where his wife and three other women would be waiting. They would unload the maize, tear the sacks open and transfer the contents to three smaller baskets. They would all carry the maize home. At home his mother-in-law would be waiting. He would give her some of the maize, pay the three women with two cans full of grain each and keep the rest for his family. The supply should keep his family going until the next trip.

It was a familiar pattern. Nothing new, nothing eventful.

Dusk.

His bull behaved well and apparently didn't need a lot to eat. He gave it some grass he had been carrying for the purpose. They walked all day, the man and the animal, until they were both exhausted by the heat. So he decided to stop under a tree for a short rest. He tied the animal to a nearby twig and lay down for a small nap. The quietness of the place lulled him into a deep sleep. How long it had lasted he couldn't quite tell. When he woke up the animal was still there but this time he was also lying down. Well, it was time to go on, so he untethered the animal and patted it on the back.

'Hey, up, up we go.'

The animal didn't budge. So he hit it slightly with a stick.

'Up, up, I say ... Get going.'

The animal remained immobile. He hit it harder. Still the animal didn't move. He grabbed its ears and pulled them. That didn't help either. He gave it two or three canes on the back. Then the animal lay on its back and began to kick in the air with froth coming from its mouth.

Kamali Lango dropped his luggage and hurried to open the animal's mouth. That proved to be quite a task. The animal gnashed its teeth and gave a groaning noise. Then there was silence.

It was a long while before the man picked up his remaining property: the stick, the torch, the wrapped-up blanket, and walked away. A battalion of vultures watched him go, and then inched nearer to the scene. They had been waiting impatiently all the while. Unlike the bull, these guardians of the sky had not succumbed yet to an epileptic fit.

Kamali Lango sombrely remembered that at Kamulamba his wife and three other women would be waiting with three baskets. He trudged home in bemused, wobbly steps.

Revision questions

1 a) How big is Kamali's family?

b) Why do you think the visit by Kamali's mother-in-law sounds a thorny issue?
2 What evidence is there that however poor Kamali is, he still hopes to improve his future?
3 It seems that the physical, social and political environment in Kamali's village all contributed to the misery of the villagers. Explain how this happened.
4 'The naked sun rose slowly and surely...'
  a) Pick out words and phrases used to describe the sun and explain what each means.
  b) Why do you think the sun is not a welcome sight in Kamali's village?
5 Make notes on Kamali's plans after he bought the bull. Did the plans materialise?
6 Discuss Kamali's character. Do you think he could have done anything else to improve his life?
7 What do you feel for people like Kamali?
8 What answer did Pancreas Mbula give the widower about the constant 'lack of rain'? What does the answer tell you about politicians?
9 'And an obstinate sonorous echo continued to ring his mind like an alarm clock'.
  a) Explain the meaning of this sentence.
  b) Pick out two more sentences that give a hint as to what will happen later.
  c) Do you find the use of suspense in this story effective?
10 What purpose does the song 'LEADER' serve in this story?
11 'The market *p*lace was bursting with *p*ompous *p*easant *p*ride, a *s*plendid *s*cene of *s*warming flie*s*, *s*corching *s*un, mooing cow*s* and *b*ellowing *b*ulls.'
  a) What do you notice about the use of letters in this sentence?
  b) What literally term do we give to such use of letters?

Topics for discussion

1 The people in this story seem to be condemned to irredeemable poverty.
  a) Discuss the theme of poverty.
  b) Is there something the people could have done to improve their lot?
2 Do the politicians in this story care for the welfare of the people?

Luis Bernado Honwana
Mozambique

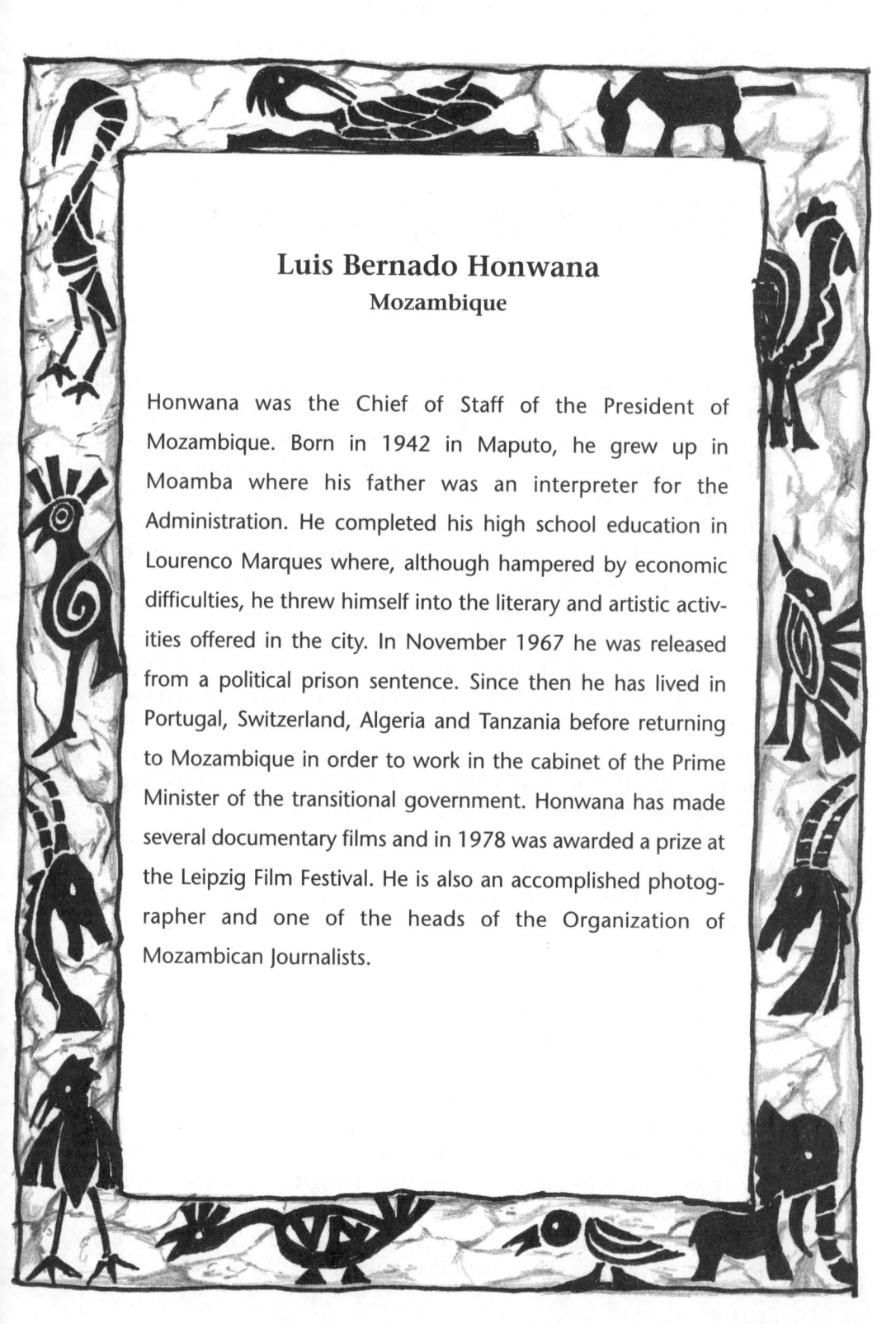

Honwana was the Chief of Staff of the President of Mozambique. Born in 1942 in Maputo, he grew up in Moamba where his father was an interpreter for the Administration. He completed his high school education in Lourenco Marques where, although hampered by economic difficulties, he threw himself into the literary and artistic activities offered in the city. In November 1967 he was released from a political prison sentence. Since then he has lived in Portugal, Switzerland, Algeria and Tanzania before returning to Mozambique in order to work in the cabinet of the Prime Minister of the transitional government. Honwana has made several documentary films and in 1978 was awarded a prize at the Leipzig Film Festival. He is also an accomplished photographer and one of the heads of the Organization of Mozambican Journalists.

The Hands of the Blacks

I don't remember now how we got onto the subject, but one day Teacher said that the palms of the blacks' hands were much lighter than the rest of their bodies because only a few centuries ago they walked around on all fours, like wild animals, so their palms were not exposed to the sun, which made the rest of their bodies darker and darker. I thought of this when Father Christiano told us after catechism that we were absolutely hopeless, and that even the blacks were better than us, and he went back to this thing about their hands being lighter, and said it was like that because they always went about with their hands folded together, praying in secret. I thought this was so funny, this thing of the blacks' hands being lighter, that you should just see me now – I don't let go of anyone, whoever they are, until they tell me why they think that the palms of the blacks' hands are lighter. Dona Dores, for instance, told me that God made their hands lighter like that so they wouldn't dirty the food they made for their masters, or anything else they were ordered to do that had to be kept quite clean.

Senhor Antunes, the Coca Cola man, who only comes to the village now and again when all the Cokes in the cantinas have been sold, said to me that everything I had been told was a lot of baloney. Of course I don't know if it was really, but he assured me it was. After I said yes, all right, it was baloney, then he told me what he knew about this thing of the blacks' hands. It was like this: 'Long ago, many years ago, God, Our Lord Jesus Christ, the Virgin Mary, St. Peter, many other saints, all the angels that were in Heaven then, and some of the people who had died and gone to Heaven – they all had a meeting and decided to make blacks. Do you know how? They got hold of some clay and pressed it into some second-hand moulds. And to bake the clay of the creatures they took them to the Heavenly kilns. Because they were in a hurry and there was no room next to the fire, they hung them in the chimneys. Smoke, smoke, smoke – and there you have them, black as coals. And now do you want to know why their hands stayed white? Well, didn't they have to hold on while their clay baked?'

Luis Bernado Honwana

The Hands of the Blacks

When he had told me this, Senhor Antunes and the other men who were around us were very pleased and they all burst out laughing. That very same day Senhor Frias called me after Senhor Antunes had gone away, and told me that everything I had heard from them there had been just one big pack of lies. Really and truly, what he knew about the blacks' hands was right – that God finished making men and told them to bathe in a lake in Heaven. After bathing the people were nice and white. The blacks, well, they were made very early in the morning, and at this hour the water in the lake was very cold, so they only wet the palms of their hands and the soles of their feet before dressing and coming into the world.

But I read in a book that happened to mention it, that the blacks have hands lighter like this because they spent their lives bent over, gathering the white cotton of Virginia and I don't know where else. Of course Dona Esterfánia didn't agree when I told her this. According to her, it is only because their hands became bleached with all that washing.

Well, I don't know what to think about all this, but the truth is that however calloused and cracked they may be, a black's hands are always lighter than all the rest of him. And that's that!

My mother is the only one who must be right about this question of a black's hands being lighter than the rest of his body. On the day that we were talking about it, us two, I was telling her what I already knew about the question, and she just couldn't stop laughing. What I thought was strange was that she didn't tell me at once what she thought about all this, and she only answered me when she was sure that I wouldn't get tired of bothering her about it. And even then she was crying and clutching herself around the stomach like someone who had laughed so much that it was quite unbearable. What she said was more or less this:

'God made blacks because they had to be. They had to be, my son. He thought they really had to be ... Afterwards He regretted having made them because the other men laughed at them and took them off to their homes and put them to serve like slaves or not much better. But because He couldn't make them all be white, for those who were used to seeing them black would complain, He made it so that the palms of their hands would be exactly like the palms of the hands of other men. And do you know why that was? Of course you don't know, and it's not surprising, because many, many people don't know. Well, listen: it was to show that what men do is only the work of men ... That what men do is done by hands that are the same – hands of people who, if they had any sense, would know that before everything else they are men.

He must have been thinking of this when He made the hands of the blacks be the same as the hands of those men who thank God they are not black!'

After telling me all this, my mother kissed my hands. As I ran off into the yard to play ball, I thought that I had never seen a person cry so much when nobody had hit them.

Revision questions
1. a) What do you think is the racial background of the child narrator?
   b) The events in this story are seen from an innocent child's perspective. Pick out and explain four examples that bring out that perspective.
2. Such colours as black, lighter and darker are mentioned in the story. What do you think is their significance?
3. This story is about racial discrimination; give four examples to show how the black people are treated.
4. Apart from the mother's explanation, each of the explanations given to the narrator signifies something negative about the blacks.
   a) What message is brought out in each example?
   b) Why is the mother's story most credible? How does it help reveal Honwana's message in this story?
5. Describe the character of the narrator. What trait in his character helps the narrator in his quest about the colour of black people's hands?

Topics for discussion
1. Why do you think the author chooses to use a child narrator in this story?
2. Comment on each of the characters that the narrator talks to about the hands of the black people.

Moyez G. Vassanji
Kenya

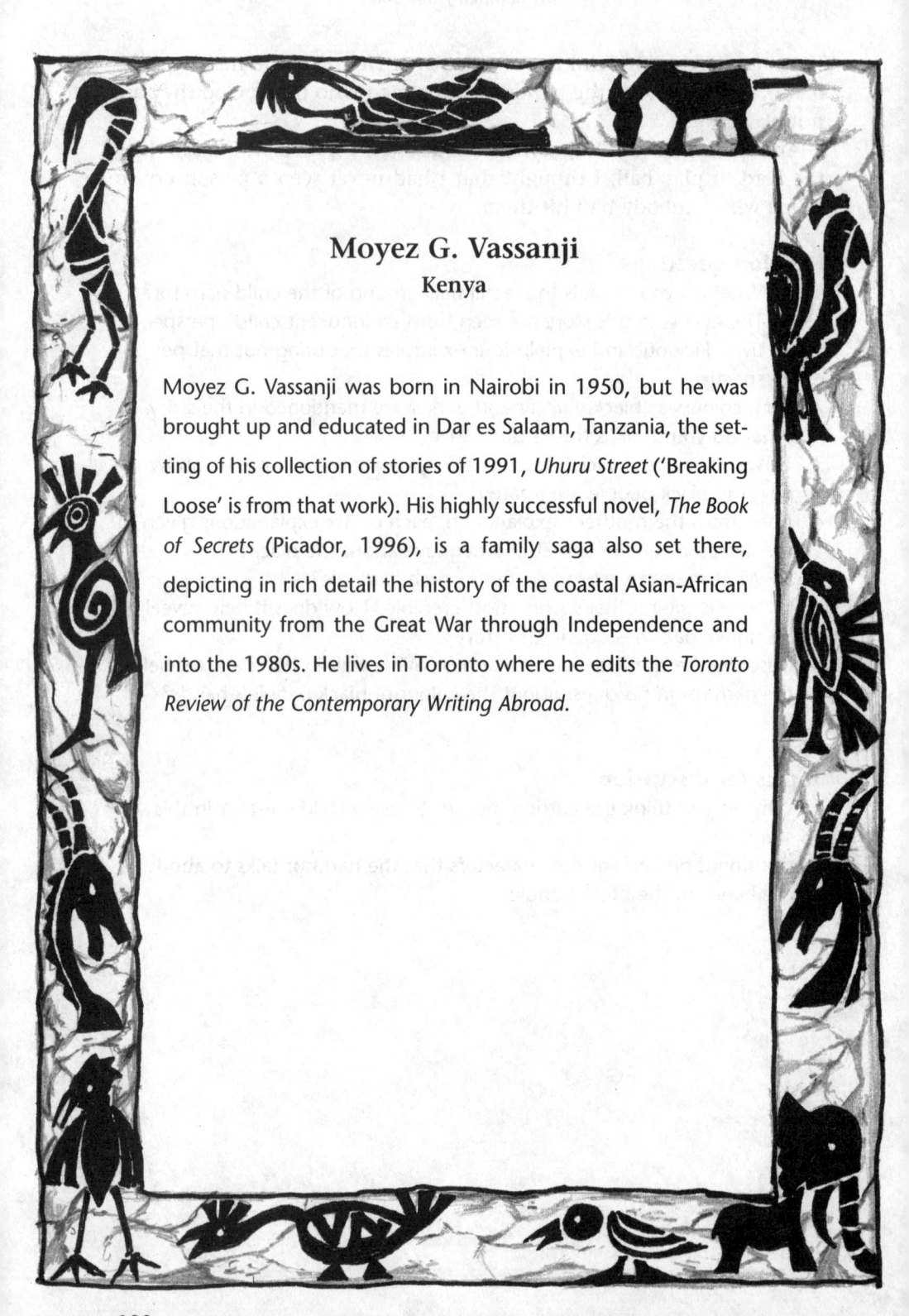

Moyez G. Vassanji was born in Nairobi in 1950, but he was brought up and educated in Dar es Salaam, Tanzania, the setting of his collection of stories of 1991, *Uhuru Street* ('Breaking Loose' is from that work). His highly successful novel, *The Book of Secrets* (Picador, 1996), is a family saga also set there, depicting in rich detail the history of the coastal Asian-African community from the Great War through Independence and into the 1980s. He lives in Toronto where he edits the *Toronto Review of the Contemporary Writing Abroad*.

Breaking Loose

The rock band, *Iblis*, was playing. The lead guitarist and singer was a local heart-throb, a young Asian with fairly long hair and bell-bottom trousers now in the midst of another brisk number from the foreign pop-charts. Close to the stage danced a group of modish, brightly dressed girls, proclaiming by their various excesses their closeness with the four band members.

Yasmin was at the far end of the dance floor with her girlfriends. Three of them occupied the table with the only chairs available, Yasmin and the other two stood around. Occasionally she would look up to take in the dance scene, the band, the modish girls, hoping to catch a vacated chair she could bring over. The band was loud, the room hot and stuffy, and the men were drenched with sweat and the girls fanning themselves with handkerchiefs or anything else they could find. A well-dressed black man, somewhat odd in a grey suit, his necktie rakishly loosened, emerged from the throng of dancing couples and went up to her requesting the dance. She went.

Of all the girls here, why me? I don't want to dance. I can't dance. From the centre of the dance floor where he'd taken her she threw a longing glance at her gang chatting away in the distance.

'I am sorry,' he smiled. 'I took you away from your friends ...'

'It's okay ... only for a few minutes –' she began and blushed, realising that unwittingly she'd agreed. After all it's an honour, she thought. He's a professor.

It was a dance that did not require closeness or touching – and she was grateful for that mercy.

'Daniel Akoto. That's my name.'

'I know ... I'm Yasmin Rajan.'

It's all so unnecessary. I'm not the type. He should have tried one of those cheeky ones dancing barefoot. Now that would have drawn some fun.

She looked at her partner. He was graceful, much more – she was certain – than she.

She was a head shorter than him. Her long hair was combed back straight and supported with a red band, in the manner favoured by schoolgirls, and she wore a simple dress. This was the middle of her second year at the University.

'Good music,' he said.

'Yes isn't it? I know the head guitarist ...'

'But too Western, don't you think?'

'I don't know ...'

She felt oppressed by the ordeal, and the heat, and the smoke, the vapours of sweat, beer and perfume. There was the little worry too – why had he picked her and would he pursue her. He was looking at her. He was offended by her attitude and going on about Asians.

'...truly colonised ... mesmerised ... more so than the African I dare say.'

She didn't reply, trying her best to give a semblance of grace to her movements – feeling guilty, wholly inadequate and terribly embarrassed.

Just when she thought the rest of the dance would proceed smoothly – the music was steady and there was a kind of lull in the noise level – the leader of the band let out a whoop from the stage. There were whoops of rejoinder followed by renewed energy on the dance floor. Akoto shook his head, and Yasmin watched him with dread.

'Look at that. *Beatniks*. Simply aping the Europeans ... not a gesture you'll find original. Your kinsmen, I presume?'

She forced a smile. *I hope he doesn't raise a scene.*

'There are African bands too, you know,' she said.

'But the *beat*, my dear, the *music*. Now take that song. *Rolling Stones*. What do you call *Indian* in that ... for instance?' he persisted. 'Perhaps I'm missing something.'

Oh why doesn't he stop, for God's sake.

'What do you mean we're colonised?' she said, exasperated. 'Of course we have our own culture. Come to our functions and see. We have centuries-old traditions ...'

She had stopped dancing and there were tears in her eyes. She felt trapped and under attack in the middle of the couple of hundred people twisting and shaking around her. She could feel curious eyes burning upon her, watching her embarrassment.

She left Akoto in the middle of the dance floor and walked stiffly to her friends.

★ ★ ★

The next day she waited for the axe to fall. A call to the vice chancellor's office, a reprimand for publicly insulting a distinguished professor, a visitor from another African country. Perhaps she would just be blacklisted: a rude Asian girl, who doesn't know her place.

During lunch in the refectory one of her friends pointed him out to her. He was standing at the door, throwing sweeping looks across the hall searching for someone. She drew a deep breath and waited. His eyes found her and he hurried forward between tables, pushing aside chairs, grinning, answering courtesies on the way with waves and shouts. When he arrived, a place was made for him at the table at which he sank comfortably, putting both his hands in front of him. He looked at her.

'About last night ...' he began. The other girls picked up their trays and left.

She laughed. 'You pushed them out,' she said. 'They'll hate you for that.'

Where had she found her confidence? He was in a red T-shirt – expensive, she thought. He looked handsome – and harmless.

'But not for long, I hope,' he began. His grin widened as he looked at her. 'Again, I've removed you from your friends – but this time I've come to apologise. I'm sorry about last night. I asked you for a dance and then played a tiresome little radical.'

'It's okay. I'm at fault too. You see ...'

'I know, I know. An innocent Indian girl in a den of wolves. But tell me – surely you expect men to come and ask you to dance in such a situation?'

She smiled, a little embarrassed. 'Usually the presence of girlfriends is enough to deter men one doesn't know ...'

'Trust a foreigner not to know the rules.' He smiled ruefully. 'You came to have a good time with your friends and I spoilt it for you. Honestly I'm sorry. Look: let me make up for it. I'll take you for a drink. How about that?'

'But I don't drink ... alcohol, I mean.'

'Tut-tut! We'll find something for you.'

He should not, of course, have pressed. But, as he said, he didn't know the rules. That's what she told herself when she found that she had accepted his invitation without any qualms.

'I'll take you to *The Matumbi*,' he said when they met later that afternoon. *The Matumbi* was a tea shop under a tree, half a mile from the campus. It had a thatched roof that only partly shaded it, and no walls. She went in hesitantly, feeling a little shy and out of place. But apparently Akoto was one of the regulars. He motioned to the owner who came up and wiped a sticky table for them, and then he pulled up a rickety chair for her, dusting it with a clean handkerchief.

'Are you hungry?' he asked.

'No. I will just have tea ... perhaps a small cake ...'

'Righto! Two teas, one cake and one *sikisti*!' he called out.

She raised an eyebrow when the *sikisti* arrived. It was an egg omelette between two inch-thick slices of bread.

'It's called *sikisti* because of its price. Sixty cents!'

She laughed.

'That's the truth, believe me!'

Akoto was a professor of sociology, on loan from the government of Ghana.

'What is your major?' he asked her after some time. 'What subject are you taking?'

'Literature.'

'Literature?'

'Yes.' *Now he thinks we are all shopkeepers.*

'Tell me: any African writers?'

'Yes. Soyinka ... Achebe ...'

'Things fall apart ...'

'The centre cannot hold.'

He laughed. 'Ngugi? Palangyo? Omari?'

She shook her head. She hadn't heard of them.

'Local writers. Budding. You should read Omari. Nuru Omari. She writes about the Coast – your territory. *Wait for Me*; that's her first book. I could lend it to you if you want.'

'It's okay ... I'll borrow it from the library.'

He looked astonished. 'But it will take time before the library acquires it.'

'I'll wait ... I don't have much time right now.'

'All right.' He was miffed.

'Now that I have made up for my rudeness,' he said at last, seeing her a little restless, 'I hope – having apologised and so on – perhaps we can go.'

I am studying literature and I have no time to read the most recent books. She felt guilty.

☆ ☆ ☆

When she saw him again it was after several days and he did not appear to notice her. He's got my message, she thought. I am not interested. Why did I go to the tea shop with him, then? ...Because he's so different. What confidence, what grace ... so Westernised ... aping the Europeans ... mesmerised ... what about him? All that external polish: he was a proper English gentleman himself! She would tell him so!

'Dear Professor Akoto,' she wrote, 'I wanted to tell you something. I thought I should tell it to you before I forget it completely. You called us Asians colonised. We are mesmerised with the West, you said. Well, have you observed yourself carefully lately? All those European mannerisms, language, clothes – suits even in hot weather: you are so much the English gentleman yourself! Yours sincerely, Yasmin Rajan. P.S. Could I borrow Omari's *Wait for Me* from you after all? Thanx.' She slipped the note under his office door.

He repeated his previous performance at lunch-time the next day, edging out her friends from the table.

'Your point is well taken,' he said. 'Touché and so on. But I thought we had forgiven all that. Still, I don't quite agree with you. And the reason is this: I know my situation. I struggle. In any case ... Let's not argue. Let me show you my library. You can borrow any book you like.'

'You have your own library?' she murmured.

When she saw it she was dazzled. Three walls were covered with books. She had never before seen so many books belonging to one person – in a sitting room, part of the furniture as it were.

'You've read all these books?' she asked.

'Well ... I wouldn't ...'

'I envy you. You must be knowledgeable.'

'Let's not get carried away now.'

'Do you also write?'

'Yes. But nothing out yet.'

He had a theory about African literature. 'It is at present digging up the roots,' he said. And that's what he was trying to do. Dig. 'So you can understand my obsession with authenticity. Even my name is a burden, an imposition.'

At *The Matumbi* where they went that evening, she had her first *sikisti*. She talked about her background.

'My father was a pawnbroker,' she said, 'but pawnshops are no longer allowed so now he has a tailoring shop. Hardly a Westernised background...'

He smiled. 'Aren't you ever going to forgive me?'

'Tell me, do you think pawnshops are exploitative?' she asked him.

'Well they tempt the poor and they do charge awfully high interest.'

'Yes, but where else can the poor get loans? Would the banks give them? And as for the high interest – do you know the kind of things they bring to pawn off? Old watches, broken bicycles, clothes sometimes. We have these unclaimed antique gramophones at home that we can't sell.'

'Is that right? Can I look at them? I might buy one. I like old things that are out of fashion.'

'Sure you can.'

He played badminton with the Asian girls one day, bringing along a shy young man from Norway. It was at a time (though they did not tell him) when they usually went to the mosque. After the game there was a heated discussion about China. And they arranged to play the next time a little later in the evening.

One afternoon, as agreed previously, Yasmin took him to her father's shop to show him the antique gramophones. They went in his car and he dropped her off outside the shop and went to park.

When he entered the shop her father met him.

'Come in, *Bwana*. What can I get for you?'

He was a short thin man with green eyes, wearing a long white shirt over his striped pyjamas.

'I came with Yasmin,' Akoto explained in his broken Swahili.

'Yes? You want to buy something?'

'I came for a gramophone–'

'Ah, yes! The professor! Sit, sit.'

Akoto sat on the bench uncomfortably and waited, looking around inside the shop. The shelves lining the walls were filled with suiting, the glass showcases displayed shirts. Yasmin's father went about his work. The girl soon arrived from the back door carrying an old gramophone. Behind her was a servant carrying two, one on top of the other, and behind the servant followed a tall thin woman: Yasmin's mother. While her father showed Akoto the gramophones, Yasmin and her mother went back inside.

'How can you bring him here like this?' said her mother angrily. 'What will the neighbours think? And the servants? It's shameful!'

'But Mummy, he is a professor!'

'I don't care if he's a professor's father!'

When they went back to the store the purchase was completed, Akoto and her father were chatting amiably about politics. Akoto was grinning, carrying a gramophone in his arms. He looked enquiringly at her.

Outside the store a few boys and girls from the neighbourhood walked by, throwing quick, curious glances inside at the guest.

'Yasmin will stay with us tonight,' said her mother a little too loudly from the back doorway where she stood. 'She'll come back tomorrow. But she won't miss her classes – I hope that is all right.'

'Don't worry, Mama. It's perfectly all right.'

It was more than a week before they met again, briefly, in a corridor.

'Where do you eat lunch these days? You're the perfect salesman,' he said in good humour. 'You sell me an old gramophone and disappear. Are you afraid I'll return it?' She gave some excuse.

Later she returned the books she had borrowed from him and declined an invitation to *The Matumbi*.

Breaking Loose

The sight of Akoto in her shop that day had driven her mother into a fit. By the time he had left the shop hugging the gramophone she was raging with fury. 'There are no friendships with men – not with men we don't know …' she said to Yasmin.

'The world is not ready for it,' her father said quietly.

'You stay out of it!' screamed his wife. 'This is between us two.'

He remained quiet but stayed within hearing distance, measuring out cloth for his tailors. If Yasmin expected any understanding, or even a reasoned discussion with an adult, experienced voice, it was from her father. But ever since she could remember she had been her mother's business. And her mother, she believed, hated her for this, for being a girl. Yasmin was not the only child; there were three brothers. But ever since she could remember her mother was always admonishing, chiding, warning her – as if believing her capable of the worst. Now it seemed that all the horrors she had imagined possible from her daughter – against her, against the name and dignity of the family – were on the verge of coming true.

'What do you know of him?' She had been uncontrollable, obsessive, had gone on and on until she was hoarse and breathless. 'With an Asian man, even if he is evil, you know what to expect. But with him?'

At the end of the day the girl felt as if her bones had been picked dry.

Yasmin did not go to the end-of-year dance on campus. From her friends she heard of the one notable event that took place there. Professor Akoto, after sitting at a table all alone for some time and apparently after a little too much drink, had got into a brawl with Mr Sharp of the Boys' School, calling him a CIA agent. Then he'd staggered out.

★ ★ ★

India was not just the past, or the community, or even the jealous Indian communities of Dar. India was a continent, a civilisation, a political entity in the world. Only recently it had emerged from a long struggle for independence.

During the holidays Yasmin discovered her world. She read avidly about India, quizzed her father about it. India came as a revelation. Here in Africa she was an Asian, an Indian. Yet she had been a stranger to even the most recent Indian history. All she had received from her people about India were ancient customs, unchanged for generations, remotely related to the world around her. At first her acknowledgement of her origins seemed to her a reaction against Akoto, the African; yet it seemed to be harking back to the authenticity he had been talking about. In a strange and diabolical way it seemed to be bringing her closer to the man, as if what she was discovering was at his bidding, as if she had to go and discuss her findings with him, answer his challenges.

The world seemed a smaller place when she went back to the University. Smaller but exciting; teeming with people struggling, fighting, loving: surviving. And she was one of those people. People, bound by their own histories and traditions, seemed to her like puppets tied to strings: but then a new mutant broke loose, an event occurred, and lives changed, the world changed. She was, she decided, a new mutant.

Yasmin's father collapsed with a heart attack under the weight of two bolts of suiting in his shop, one month after the University reopened. A servant was dispatched to fetch a doctor, who arrived an hour and a half later. By that time the former pawnbroker had died.

Daniel Akoto attended the funeral. He sat among the men, initially on the ground, trying to fold his legs, sweating profusely, pressed from all sides. A black face in a sea of patient brown Asian faces. He was not wearing a suit, just a very clean white shirt, but this time some of the other men were in jackets. A servant saw the discomfited man and placed a chair for him against the wall adjacent to the door. Now Akoto could see clearly across the room. The body was lying on a low table behind which two men sat on the floor administering the last rites to the dead. The widow sat beside the dead man, sobbing, comforted by her daughter, occasionally breaking into a wail and joined by other women. Mrs Rajan looked away from Akoto when their eyes first met. She moaned and started weeping. She saw him again through a film of tears, lost control and gave a loud wail.

'You!' she screamed, 'what are you doing here? What kind of man are you, who comes to take away my daughter even in my grief ... Who asked you to come? Go away!' she wept.

Akoto, understanding only partly her speech but fully the intent, tried to smile apologetically at the men and women now turning to stare at him.

'Go!' said the disraught woman, pointing a finger at the door beside him.

No one else said a word. Akoto stood up, gave a respectful bow towards the dead man and left.

A week later Yasmin knocked on his door late in the evening and caught him in.

'Come in,' he said, putting away his pipe.

'I've come to apologise about that day.'

It's all right. A funeral is not exactly where people are at their best ... perhaps they are more honest though.' He eyed her.

'You could have us arrested. You could ...'

'Don't be silly! Take a hold of yourself. What do you think I am anyway – the secret police?'

'You must despise us,' she said more quietly. 'You are educated, learned ... your government has loaned you to us ... You are a great man ...'

'No, I don't despise you. And don't call me great, for God's sake.'

She began to laugh, a little hysterically. They both laughed.

'And you, I respect you.' He spoke calmly. 'You are brave. You left that gang of girls that day at the dance and since then you've done it again and again. It takes courage, what you've done, trying to break away from tribalism – that's all it is ultimately ... even coming here like this. I realise that and I like you.'

'Well, I like you too!' she said too quickly. There was a silence between them. 'You know, it's not going to be easy ... with my father dead, this will be the greatest shock to my mother ... it will kill her, it will ...'

'Now, now.' He went up to her, put her wet face on his shirt. 'We'll have to do the best we can, won't we?'

Revision questions

1. a) What do you understand by the title *Breaking Loose*?
   b) From what are Yasmin Rajan and Prof. Akoto breaking loose?
2. In what way can Yasmin and Prof. Akoto claim to be true adherents of their respective cultures?
3. 'Why did I go to the tea shop with him, then?' Give four examples to show that Yasmin was attracted to Prof. Akoto.
4. How did Yasmin's parents react to their daughter's relationship with the professor?
5. a) Why do you think Yasmin took time to seriously read about her country, India?
   b) How did her new knowledge help change her attitude on racial issues?
6. a) Discuss the character of Yasmin and Prof. Akoto in detail.
   b) What do you find common in the two characters?
   c) Identify two other characters from the story and discuss them.
7. Vivid descriptions and rich use of dialogue are the two main stylistic devices applied in this story. Discuss each.

Topics for discussion

1. In this story three types of relationships are clearly portrayed, namely:
   a) racial relations
   b) family relations

c) romantic relations.
Show how each of them is portrayed.
2 What lessons do you learn from this story?
3 'You know, it's not going to be easy ... We'll have to do the best we can, won't we?'
The story does not end on a happy note for Yasmin and Prof. Akoto.
a) What do you imagine they did about their love affair?
b) Give your own opinion about the affair.